Jonquils for Jax

THE ROUSSEAUS, BOOK #1
THE BLUEBERRY LANE SERIES

KATY REGNERY

SPENCER
HILL
PRESS

Excerpt from the poem "a song in the front yard" in *Selected Poems* (1963) by Gwendolyn Brooks. *Reprinted By Consent of Brooks Permissions.*

Please visit www.katyregnery.com

First Edition: August 2016
Katy Regnery

Jonquils for Jax: a novel / by Katy Regnery—1st ed.
ISBN: 978-1-63392-092-7

Library of Congress Cataloging-in-Publication Data available upon request

Published in the United States by Spencer Hill Press
This is a Spencer Hill Contemporary Romance, Spencer Hill
Contemporary is an imprint of Spencer Hill Press.
For more information on our titles visit www.spencerhillpress.com

Distributed by Midpoint Trade Books
www.midpointtrade.com

Cover design by: Marianne Nowicki
Interior layout by: Scribe, Inc.
The World of Blueberry Lane Map designed by: Paul Siegel

Printed in the United States of America

The Blueberry Lane Series

THE ENGLISH BROTHERS

Breaking Up with Barrett
Falling for Fitz
Anyone but Alex
Seduced by Stratton
Wild about Weston
Kiss Me Kate
Marrying Mr. English

THE WINSLOW BROTHERS

Bidding on Brooks
Proposing to Preston
Crazy about Cameron
Campaigning for Christopher

THE ROUSSEAUS

Jonquils for Jax
Marry Me Mad
J.C. and the Bijoux Jolis

THE STORY SISTERS

The Bohemian and the Businessman
2017
The Director and Don Juan
2017
The Flirt and the Fox
2017
The Saint and the Scoundrel
2017

THE AMBLERS

Two novels
Coming 2018

Based on the best-selling series by Katy Regnery,

The World of...

The Rousseaus of Chateau Nouvelle
Jax, Mad, J.C.
Jonquils for Jax • Marry Me Mad
J.C and the Bijoux Jolis

The Story Sisters of Forrester
Priscilla, Alice, Elizabeth, Jane
Coming Summer 2017

The Winslow Brothers of Westerly
Brooks, Preston, Cameron, Christopher
Bidding on Brooks • Proposing to Preston
Crazy About Cameron • Campaigning for Christopher

The Amblers of Greens Farms
Bree, Dash, Sloane
Coming Summer 2018

The English Brothers of Haverford Park
Barrett, Fitz, Alex, Stratton, Weston, Kate
Breaking up with Barrett • Falling for Fitz
Anyone but Alex • Seduced by Stratton
Wild about Weston • Kiss Me Kate
Marrying Mr. English

For Amy and Mia.
Because when I wrote the scenes with Jax, Skye, and Daisy,
I was wishing it was us.
xo

CONTENTS

I've stayed in the front yard all my life.
I want a peek at the back
Where it's rough and
untended and hungry
weed grows.
A girl gets sick of a rose.

—Gwendolyn Brooks
from *"a song in the front yard" Selected Poems* (1963)

Chapter 1

Jax Rousseau had been thinking a lot about destiny lately.

Hers in particular.

What did she want from life, and what if what she *wanted* was different from whatever the universe had already *fated* her to receive? Because it really and truly felt like the universe was *not* on her side.

"Jaxy-baby, wait up!"

"No," she muttered, quickening her pace, her hands starting to sweat as he chased her across the lawn. Not to mention . . . *Jaxy?* She gagged a little. *As if.*

After ducking through the hedgerow that separated her childhood home, Le Chateau, from her neighbor's estate, Westerly, she peeked over her shoulder to see if Tripp was still weaving unsteadily behind her and sighed with relief when she didn't see him. She slowed her pace as she walked farther into the dark shadows of Westerly's gardens.

Tripp Stuyvesant Stanton IV wasn't even her date; he'd just been seated beside her at the wedding reception of Jax's older brother, Étienne. And she didn't like Tripp all that much, though her mother had probably handpicked him as Jax's dinner companion since he was, as Liliane Rousseau liked to remind her daughter, one of the "right" people.

Jax reached down for a bright-white peony and picked it, lifting it to her nose and breathing deeply.

The thing is, the "right" people had always felt wrong.

She knew dozens of guys like Tripp: wealthy, well-bred guys from good Philadelphia families who worked for their fathers' law firms or grandfathers' hedge fund. They'd gone to the right prep schools, followed by an Ivy League education. She'd foxtrotted with them in ballroom dance classes since the third grade and ridden against them in polo matches since high school. She ran into them at the Merion Cricket Club every July, at The Union League Club Christmas party every December, and at the Cos (a.k.a. The Cosmopolitan Club, which was her generation's co-ed answer to the stiff and matronly Acorn), where Jax had been a luncheon regular before she moved to LA.

In fact, Tripp had escorted Mad, Jax's twin sister, to junior cotillion, and—she glanced up at the mostly dark windows of the Winslows' Westerly as she continued across the lawn—he had crewed for Brooks Winslow in a regatta more than once. And let us not forget, she thought acidly, that Tripp was set to inherit his family's millions, and as the only child, he wouldn't have to share.

He was also a boring conversationalist, a high-handed dinner partner, and a handsy drunk, and he didn't know how to take no for an answer.

Being chased like this a year ago, before her unfortunate sojourn in Hollywood, probably wouldn't have bothered her as much. She would have just rolled her eyes at him and told him to get lost. But a lot had happened since last year. Tripp's persistent pursuit was bringing up the worst memories of Jax's time in LA and setting her on edge.

"Jax? Jaxy! C'mon, gor . . . jus!" he called from behind her. "*Voooly voo coochie 'vec moi*? Jaaaaaa-xy!"

He chuckled like his pigeon French was hilarious, and though his voice wasn't close, she could tell he'd made it through the hedgerow into Westerly because it wasn't muffled by the wall of shrubbery. Jax hurried her steps, picking up the skirt of her bridesmaid dress and trying not to twist her ankle in four-inch, gold Manolo Blahnik "Chaos Cuff" sandals as she ran over the uneven grass. She darted through the gate that separated Westerly from Haverford Park, the English family's estate, and latched it behind her. Still looking over her shoulder to catch a glimpse of Tripp—*oooof!*—she slammed into a wall of something.

"Whoa there!" said a man's voice.

"Hey!" she cried.

Teetering for a moment on her heels, she lost the battle with gravity and landed with an inelegant plop on her satin, champagne-colored backside, the cold dampness of the dew-covered grass making her suck in a gasp of breath as she looked up in alarm.

In the moonlight, she could make out the silhouette of a giant whose head partially blocked the full moon.

"You okay, miss?" he asked, leaning down to offer her his hand.

She really didn't want to take it—she not only blamed him wholeheartedly for her fall, but it was dark, and his sudden presence set off a carillon of warning bells in her head. Then again, getting up on four-inch heels required either a hand or flipping to all fours. And she was *not* getting on all fours in front of this . . . this . . .

"Who are you?" she asked, having no other option but to reach for his hand.

"Who are *you*?"

He wore battered leather gloves, which chafed her palm as he pulled her to her feet and added to her apprehension. Gloves. Why gloves? He clearly wasn't a wedding guest, so why was he lurking around her neighbor's estate at ten o'clock at night? Her heart sped up with uneasiness as she regained her balance. She jerked her hand back and took a huge step away from him.

The stranger stood still before her. He was over six feet tall and broad-chested—she wouldn't have a chance in hell of defending herself against him if he chose to make a move on her. Suddenly, drunk, handsy Tripp, who had a muffin-top spilling over the waistband of his Vineyard Vines khakis, didn't seem so bad.

She flicked a glance over her shoulder and lifted her chin, forcing bravado, wondering how far her voice would carry if she had to scream. "You don't look like a wedding guest."

"That's 'cause I'm not," he said, his voice calm, his drawl slightly Southern.

She took another step back. "Then what are you doing here at the Englishes' estate in the dark?"

She glanced at his hands, looking for the glow of a concealed a camera, but she didn't see one. That didn't mean anything, though. He could be recording their exchange. He could have a camera hidden. He could—

"I'm Gardener," he said, offering her his hand.

"The gardener?"

This information took the edge off of her worry. He was the gardener? Well, gardeners were, more or less, "safe" on Blueberry Lane. They were "the help," and the help didn't attack wedding guests or gossip or take pictures to sell to magazines, because they were paid not only to do their jobs but also for their discretion. Jax had lived her life surrounded by friendly gardeners, chauffeurs, maids, housekeepers, and cooks, so there was a certain solid comfort to his claim. Except—

She scowled at him, crossing her arms in a refusal to shake his hand. "I've lived in this neighborhood forever, and you are *not* the gardener at Haverford Park."

"Is that right?" he drawled, a slight thread of humor warming his voice. Was he laughing at her? It sort of sounded like it, though a cloud had stalled over the moon and it was too dark for her to see his face to confirm it.

"Felix Edwards is the gardener here," she said with a sniff, "and right now he's over at Le Chateau with everyone else."

"Sounds 'bout right."

God damn it, if some smarmy paparazzo somehow managed to take pictures of me dancing with Tripp or stumbling through Westerly in the dark, or . . . or . . . merde! Why can't they leave me the hell alone?

"Why are you *really* here?" she asked, her tone of voice rising with a lot of anger, a good dose of frustration, and more than a little growing panic. "Who the hell *are* you?"

"Gardener," he said again, his voice soft and even.

Jax clenched her jaw, just about ready to run back to Le Chateau, when the cloud passed and the moonlight illuminated his face and form. Despite her apprehension, she couldn't resist checking him out for an extra moment, trying to figure out who he was and why he was here.

He was wearing jeans and a dark-colored T-shirt under an open plaid flannel shirt. Cream-colored leather work boots and yellow leather gloves rounded out his outfit. Pausing at his hand, she found he was holding something and stiffened. She craned her neck, but upon further inspection, she realized that it wasn't a camera or tape recorder as she'd feared. It was a seedling—a young plant cradled in the palm of his glove.

Huh. *Was* he the gardener as he claimed?

She flicked her eyes back to his face and was surprised to find him staring at her, a very slight grin on his perfect lips, which, for no good reason, annoyed her.

"We're not getting anywhere," she said, scowling at him and ignoring the drunken call of "Jaxy" in the distance. "If

Felix is the gardener at Haverford Park, then who are *you* and what are *you* doing here?"

His grin widened just a touch and he shook his head like she was funny.

"Shhhh," he said. "You'll scare the flowers."

Scare the flowers? She blinked at him.

Was he crazy? Some crazy cousin of the English brothers who gardened at night? *Merde.* She'd jumped from the frying pan into the flame. What was worse? A drunken admirer who was trying to sleep with her? Or a crazy stranger who thought plants had feelings? Hmm. It was a toss-up.

"Jaaaaaa-xy!"

She took another step back, half grateful that Tripp's calls were closer now. "Scare . . . the flowers."

He nodded. "You're yellin', Duchess."

Duchess? Huh. Duchess. She cocked her head to the side, surprised to find she didn't dislike this nickname half as much as she probably should. Something about the way he said it in his low Southern drawl was almost . . . sexy. Disarming. And incredibly distracting.

She cleared her throat and shook her head, saying in a loud whisper, "I'm *not* yelling."

"Sorta you are," he said, turning his back to her and walking a few paces away.

As she trailed him with her eyes, she realized, for the first time, that she was standing at the edge of a formal garden and that the flowers before her were . . . glowing. White and silver in the moonlight, petals of all shapes and sizes reached for the starry sky, drinking in the moonlight and transforming themselves into nature's version of twinkle lights.

She sucked in an admiring breath, taking her first step forward but still keeping a white stone bench between her and the "gardener," who had dropped to his knees to plant the seedling. He bent over the blueish-white border of flowers, concentrating on his work, ignoring her.

"What—what is this place?" she asked with quiet wonder so she wouldn't scare the flowers.

He turned to look at her over his shoulder, his small smile still in place. "It's a moonlight garden."

Lord but Northern girls are brassy, thought Gardener, and this one, God help him, was jumpy and bossy too. Though, if he was being honest . . . the way she looked in the moonlight? With her dark hair piled up on her head, held back with a diamond tiara, and that long, gold dress that hugged the curves of her body like a glove? Well, she had him thinking about more than gardening.

He'd started working around six o'clock and had been listening to the wedding revelry float on the warm June breeze from Le Chateau to Haverford Park all evening long. Sounded like a good party. The kind he used to enjoy.

Using his gloved hand, he scooped a bit more earth from the hole he'd dug, then gently placed the lavender plant into the void before pushing the soil back over the seedling roots. The purple of the tight petals wouldn't add much to the night glow of brighter flowers like white jonquils, Purity cosmos, Miss Jekyll White nigella, white larkspur, and the annual white foxglove Excelsior he'd planted a few nights ago, but the smell of the herb, when mixed with the night-scented stock that he planned to start planting tomorrow evening, would add a great deal of olfactory beauty to the garden on a hot summer night. His father would have approved, he thought wistfully.

The duchess cleared her throat behind him and he looked over his shoulder at her again, but he didn't let his gaze linger. He couldn't see her all that well anyhow, but her body language told him that she was uncomfortable finding herself alone with him. More than uncomfortable. Rattled.

And yet, he thought, for all her agitation, she'd still stood there in the dark giving him "what-for" and the third degree. She had spirit in her too. Because he hoped it might ease her anxiety, he knelt down and went about his business, though part of him, the *stupid* part, hoped she wouldn't leave right away. It had been a lonely night before her arrival.

"A moonlight garden," she said, her voice a little gentler and less uptight than it had been before. "It's very—"

"Jaaaaaa-xy!"

Gardener heard the man's voice in the distance again. Sounded like a neighbor searching for his dog, Jackie. Gardener looked up, scanning the darkness behind the woman but seeing nothing, even with the full moonlight shining down. He wouldn't be any good helping someone find a dog. Couldn't see but a foot in front of him on a good day with full sunlight, let alone nighttime, when he was as good as blind.

"Does somebody in this neighborhood *where you've lived forever* have a dog named Jackie?" he asked. "Sounds like it mighta went missin'."

She huffed with annoyance, and when he looked up, she had her hands on her hips and a puss on her face. "*I'm* Jaxy."

It was on the tip of his tongue to point out that she wasn't a dog, but thank the Lord he held back. "You're name . . . is *Jaxy*?"

"No!" She inhaled a deep breath, then released it. "It's Jacqueline. My friends call me Jax."

In the past year or so, his ears had started making up for what his eyes had lost, and if he wasn't mistaken, he heard a slight accent in the pronunciation of her full name. French. And like every other good Cajun boy, he could still pick it out with ease, no matter how many years it had been since he'd been home.

"So, who's callin' you Jaxy?"

"Just a—none of your business."

"Fair 'nough," he said, returning to his work.

He used a spade to dig another hole about three inches from the one he'd just filled, smoothing the inside with his gloved hand before standing up and rounding the bench where she was sitting. He leaned down, picked up another seedling from the crate, and walked back around her without saying a word.

"He's not my boyfriend," she said in a tight voice.

"I wasn't askin'," he said softly, pulling the small heap of soil over the lavender and brushing off its tough petals.

"My mother sat me next to him. At my brother's wedding."

Sister of the groom? He looked up. Well, that explained the accent. She was one of the Rousseaus from the ostentatiously named Le Chateau two doors down.

"*Félicitations*," he offered reflexively, the word sounding rusty to his ears.

"*M-Merci*," she answered, her voice surprised. After a moment she asked, "*Parlez-vous français?*"

"Not much anymore," he said, picking up the spade and digging another small hole.

"You're not French from France," she said, a superior sniff in her tone.

"Got that right, Duchess," he said, stepping around the bench again to take another lavender seedling. But this time he stopped in front of her, looking down and squinting to make her out as best he could. Dark hair. Long neck. Big tits. Small waist. Stupid shoes.

Duchesse Rousseau.

"Don't you have a weddin' to attend?" he asked.

"Jaaaaaa-xy! I never banged a Holl'wood c'lebrity. C'mon. Where t'fuck are you?"

She sucked in an audible breath, and Gardener snapped his head up to look into the blank of darkness. He couldn't see anything, but he wrinkled his nose and narrowed his eyes. *Never did like it much when a grown man cursed at a lady . . . even if she is brassy, bossy, and uptight.*

"Real winner you got there," he said dryly, getting back to work.

"I don't '*got*' him. I told you, he's *not* my boyfriend," she said, standing up in a huff. She tottered for a moment before regaining her balance, and Gardener rolled his eyes. *Fashion over function. Ridiculous.*

"Right," he said, squatting down beside the herb bed. When he looked over his shoulder a moment later, she was still standing there, looking in the direction of the asshole who was beckoning her oh-so-sweetly. Shaking his head with annoyance, he stood up and wiped his gloved hands on the thighs of his jeans. "Want me to walk you back to your party?"

"Absolutely not," she scoffed, looking away from him before clearing her throat and raising her chin. "I don't even know you."

"Fine," he grumbled, feeling like an idiot for suggesting it and starting to wish she'd just go already and leave him the hell alone.

"Well," she said, her voice uncertain. "I guess I'll go now."

He didn't answer. He planted the next damned seedling and covered it with soil.

"It was nice . . ." He assumed she didn't finish with "to meet you" because, one, it hadn't been all that nice, and two, they hadn't actually met.

"Good-bye," she muttered.

He looked up to see her pick up her skirt and walk into the darkness, something pulling at his heart as her lithe body disappeared into the void. Should he go after her? Shadow her from a distance until he knew she was safe? He growled softly with irritation, standing up and looking around.

Blackness. Sheer blackness but for the shimmery light of the white flowers in a semicircle around him and a dim patio light, off to the far right, on the front porch of the small studio apartment where he was staying.

Even if he wanted to follow her, it wasn't an option. He lived in a world of shadows, and though his eyes bothered him a lot less at night, he didn't see any better.

Sighing, he turned back to his work. He still had ten more lavender seedlings to plant before mulching and watering the bed and cleaning up. Another hour of work at least.

"Jax! Where the *fuck* you hidin'?" The voice was a good bit closer now.

"*Merde*," Gardener grumbled, the curse word coming easily, though he hadn't uttered it in years. She was wandering around somewhere in the darkness on stilts, trying to avoid this drunken asshole. Dumb girl. Foolish girl. Girl about to get herself hurt. He stood up, his useless eyes scanning the night.

He couldn't see a thing.

It was the sound of her scream that led him to her.

Chapter 2

Jostling.

Like being in a wagon or on a hayride.

Jax opened her eyes and saw the moon racing across the sky, the stars a blur. Hot breath landed in rough pants across her cheek. Not a wagon. Someone's arms. She was in someone's arms and he was running.

"Where am—?"

Her words were like a gong crashing around in her skull, loud and angry. She gasped in surprise and winced, reaching up to touch her temple. Her fingers landed in something warm and sticky. When she drew back her hand and looked at her fingers in the darkness; they were shiny and black.

"Hold tight," he rasped. "We'll be there in a minute."

There? She risked a question, despite the pain, grimacing as the word left her mouth. "Where?"

"Gardener's cottage."

The gardener's cottage. At Le Chateau? Or . . . no. At Haverford Park. *It's a moonlight garden.* Right. The new gardener.

"You can . . ." She winced. ". . . put me down."

"Not a chance, Duchess," he said, though he slowed down a little. He still walked purposefully, however, his long legs eating the ground between them and the cottage.

She looked over his shoulder as they passed the glowing white garden where he'd been working. Right. He'd been working in the garden and she'd bumped into him. They'd talked for a few minutes. Then she'd left him to go back to the party, and—

Tripp.

Tripp had stopped her during her walk back across Westerly, holding her arm too hard to keep her from continuing. She'd told him to let go and he'd refused, pulling her against his body. As he tried to kiss her, she'd bitten his lip and he'd shoved her away roughly. She fell to the grass and hit her head on something hard. Then? Darkness.

"Was it a rock?" she asked, reaching for her temple again.

"Corner of the patio over at Westerly. Comin' back to you now?"

"A . . . little."

His voice was terse when he said, "If you hadn't screamed, Lord only knows what might have happen—"

"I screamed?"

"Luckily," he muttered.

Still holding her securely with one arm, he reached for the doorknob and opened it, stepping into a dim, cool room and leaving the door to the outside open. Gently, he lowered her to a couch, then stood over her, giant and disapproving in the light of a reading lamp that cast the room in a soft glow.

He took his gloves off, placing them on the coffee table between them, then shrugged out of his flannel shirt and draped it next to the gloves. Pulling one wrist over his head, he bent his arm and stretched it, grunting softly with pleasure as the joint cracked, and she suddenly realized exactly how far he'd had to carry her.

"Don't move," he muttered. "I need to check your head."

From where she lay on the couch, Jax watched him turn away and step through a white-painted door at the far side of the room. When he flicked on the wall light, she could see a white toilet and sink. Clean and tidy.

It was the first time she'd had a chance to check him out in any sort of reliable light. With his back to her, she ogled him freely as he squatted down in front of the cabinets under the sink, his long legs compressing and his jeans slipping down a little to show a strip of his lower back between his waistband and T-shirt. Pronounced tan line. Mmm.

His dark-blond hair was a little too long and curled at the ends, covering the back of his neck and brushing the neckline of his T-shirt. It was thick and wavy and her fingers itched to know what it would feel like threaded between them.

She sighed, leaning back and staring up at the ceiling as she tried to figure out exactly where she was. There must be a studio apartment attached to the back of Felix Edwards' garden cottage, she decided, closing her eyes. And Eleanora English had certainly outfitted it with a very comfortable couch . . .

A light smacking on her cheek made her eyes fly open. "No closin' those emeralds, Duchess."

He was kneeling on the floor beside her, his face close— *very* close, almost *too* close—as he inspected the wound on her temple. His eyes were dark brown, and his eyelashes, almost black, were long, straight, and unreasonably thick (or unfairly so, at least, for a man). His nose was long and patrician and his lips, light pink and slightly chapped, were flumed and full. She took a deep breath, and soil, lavender, and leather made for such an unexpectedly appealing combination of smells, she had to fight against closing her eyes again. Or sighing.

No more sighing. She was sighing altogether too much around this man.

She flattened her hands on either side of her hips, intending to sit up, but he placed a rough, warm palm on her bare skin, below her throat, above the neckline of her dress, pressing down lightly on her chest as he shook his head. "Nope. You're not leavin' yet."

Panic sluiced through her veins, immediate and shocking. His lips parted and his eyes darted to his hand, which he lifted like her skin was on fire. He leaned back from her, putting both of his hands up, palms out.

"No harm meant. Just . . . don't sleep and don't bolt up. You were unconscious for a few minutes there. I'm worried about a possible concussion. Breathe. Give yourself a minute, okay? I wouldn't have saved you if my intention was to hurt you, *Jacqueline*."

His voice was warm. Soft and gentle. And the way he said "Jacqueline" with his indecipherable accent—like a very, very rough and naughty version of how her Parisian-born family said it—she sighed. Again. *Merde.* But she couldn't help it.

I wouldn't have saved you if my intention was to hurt you.

Part of her knew she shouldn't trust him—knew that men could make you trust them only to take dirty pictures of you and post them all over the Internet, or charm you into letting your defenses down so you'd say something they could take out of context and use against you. But this man . . . well, she didn't know why she trusted him, but she did. Something about him just felt safe. She looked into his dark-brown eyes, searching them for only a moment before nodding.

"I believe you."

"Then let me tend to your head, huh?"

He reached for the reading lamp and refocused it on her forehead, squinting as he cleaned the cut with a soft cloth and warm water. She was so mesmerized by his face so close to hers, the smell of alcohol didn't register immediately, but she winced with pain and cried out as he pressed the antiseptic to her temple.

"Ouch! Stop!"

"Hold still. I'm cleanin' it."

"It hurts!" she wailed.

"It's better'n gettin' an infection."

"Says you! You're not the one being tortured."

"Tortured." He chuckled softly, rolling his eyes. "Hardly, Duchess."

Finally he smoothed a Band-Aid over the cut, taking a deep breath and sighing as he stared at his work, his face less than an inch from hers. As she watched him, his eyes slid from her injury to meet her gaze and her heart skipped a beat.

"What, um, what is this place?"

His tongue darted out to wet his lips as he leaned away from her. "Apartment attached to the back of the gardener's cottage."

Now that he'd drawn away, she missed having him so close.

"You're . . . staying here?" she asked.

"For now."

She cleared her throat. "Can I sit up now?"

"Go crazy," he said, looking into her eyes for a moment before standing up. He leaned down and gathered the cloth, container of alcohol, and box of Band-Aids together before returning them to the bathroom.

Jax sat up slowly, lowering her feet to the floor and realizing that she only had one shoe on. "Where's my other shoe?"

The gardener turned around in the bathroom doorway, crossing his arms over his massive chest as his nostrils flinched into a slight sneer. "With your . . . *friend.* I guess."

With two older brothers, Jax was accustomed to swearing, but she'd never heard Jean-Christian or Étienne say "fuck" as darkly as this man had just uttered the word "friend."

"He wanted a kiss," she murmured.

"Guessin' you didn't have one to give?"

"I do, actually . . . I *do* have one to give," she whispered, the words coming from nowhere she recognized as she held his eyes from across the room. "But not to him."

The stranger's eyes widened, then narrowed, his large body still as he searched her face. Suddenly, he dropped her gaze and sighed. "C'mon, Duchess, I'll walk you back to Le Chateau."

Jax's cheeks flushed hot as a sound like a plane crashing reverberated through her aching head. Ugh. What the heck was she doing? Making passes at strange men—at strange *gardeners*, no less—wasn't exactly commonplace for Jax. She wasn't given to seduction, and she wasn't very good at it. Obviously.

"No, thanks," she said, embarrassed beyond belief. Thanking God that Kate English had chosen bridesmaids' gowns that included deep pockets, she fished around in hers for her phone. "I'll call my brother to come and get me."

Without waiting for the man to say anything, she turned her back to him and dialed Jean-Christian's cell. It rang six times before he answered.

"What?" His voice was breathy, as though he'd just run a mile or just finished—

"Jean-Christian?" she squeaked.

"This better be good, Jax," he grated out. "I'm *with* someone."

She cringed. "I'm at the gardener's cottage at Haverford Park, just inside the gates. I need you to come and get me. I lost one of my shoes. And it's dark."

"Walk. It's not even a quarter mile, *petite sœur.*"

"I'm *barefoot*," she insisted, her voice almost a whine. She didn't care if she was breaking up her brother's tryst. She'd had enough for tonight. She refused to let the gardener walk her home after rejecting her. It was way too humiliating. "Come and get me, *peigne-cul*."

"*Moi*? *I'm* the asshole? Try again," he muttered. He sighed long and hard before she heard him say to someone else, "Forgive me, but my idiot sister is stranded down the road and needs my help." He paused, then said, "*Oui!* Of course! It was a slice of heaven, *chéri*. Write down your number. I'll call you sometime soon."

"No, he won't," said Jax under her breath.

"*Tu vas fermer ta putain de gueule*," her brother growled into the phone. "I'll be there in five. You owe me."

She grinned. He'd essentially just told her to "shut the fuck up," but at least he was coming for her. And rather quickly, at that, it occurred to her. Almost like he was . . . *escaping*. Hmm.

"Maybe *you* owe *me*," she said saucily, hanging up and turning to look at the man who still stood across the room. "My brother's coming."

"I can walk you to the gate."

"Don't trouble yourself," she said, lifting her chin a little.

He rolled his eyes and sighed. "Fine."

Jax stood up, placing her phone back into her pocket before meeting his steady gaze. Even though he'd rejected her offer of a kiss, he'd also saved her from harm, carried her from Westerly to Haverford Park, and bandaged up her cut. She touched the Band-Aid on her temple. "Thank you."

He didn't say the conventional and polite "You're welcome." Instead, he looked annoyed with her and said, "Maybe find some better company."

"I told you, he's not my boyfri—"

"Or enroll yourself in a self-defense class if you're goin' to hang out with rapists."

Jax gulped. "Tripp Stanton is many things, but he's *not*—"

He took a step forward, looking at her like she was crazy. "You're goin' to defend him now?"

"He was just drunk!"

"That's no excuse! He had his hands on you! He knocked you to the ground and made you bleed! I should have punched his teeth out! I should have—" His eyes burned with rage for a long moment before he looked down, staring at the floor and fuming.

Jax's eyes widened, but instead of stepping away from the gardener's tirade, she stepped closer to him, speaking gently. "He just got drunk and made a mistake."

His head snapped up, his eyes nailing hers. "You're goin' to get hurt."

"What do you care?"

"I don't know." He shrugged, exhaling a long, deep breath before shaking his head. "Ex-cop. Force of habit . . . I guess."

Ex-cop. Huh. Ex-cop. Maybe *that's* what she'd somehow sensed . . . and why she'd trusted him: he wasn't a predator. He was a protector.

Jax ran her greedy eyes over his muscled arms and the well-defined ridges of his chest under his T-shirt. It made sense to her—the way he'd saved her, the way he'd carried her to safety and seen to her wound. He was the opposite of *everything* she'd come to fear. *An ex-cop.* She almost sighed.

"I've never met a cop before, let alone an ex-cop."

The hint of a smile softened his lips. "Not surprised, Duchess. I doubt we're invited to the same soirees."

"Why *ex*?"

He stared at her, then sighed. "None of your business."

"Jax? Ja-a-a-a-a-x? *Où es-tu?*"

Her brother was calling from the front side of the cottage. She headed to the door, feeling out of sorts about the way she was leaving things with her unlikely hero . . . like there was more to be said and she was about to lose her chance to say it.

"Why do all the men in your life yell 'Ja-a-a-a-x' when they're lookin' for you?" he asked softly from behind.

She turned to meet his eyes over her shoulder and shrugged. "They can't all call me duchess."

His lips tilted up into a smile, and she felt such a rush of victory—it was a wonder she didn't faint. God, he was beautiful. When he smiled, he was utterly and completely beautiful.

"*Bonne nuit, Jacqueline*," he said in a low rumble. It made goose bumps rise on her skin, and she gasped softly.

"*Au revoir. Merci.*"

He nodded once, lifting his hand in farewell as she slipped out the door and ran barefoot around the cottage to meet her brother.

Gardener stared at the door for what felt like an hour before finally crossing the room and lowering himself to the sofa, where she'd been lying a few minutes ago. The spot was still warm, which made him flinch, made his nostrils flare in acknowledgment. *La duchesse* was gone, but something of her remained, and it was unsettling to him.

The initial adrenaline rush from hearing her scream and finding her injured had subsided now, but he still felt wired. He needed to *do* something.

He grabbed his gloves from the coffee table and pulled them on as he headed back outside into the darkness. Kneeling down in the grass by the border, he dug three new holes for the last three lavender seedlings, but his mind wandered endlessly as he worked. The peace he'd found working in the moonlight garden an hour ago, before meeting Jacqueline Rousseau, was elusive now.

A decent cover of *Fly Me to the Moon* by the wedding band floated over from Le Chateau on the breeze, accompanied by the clink of champagne glasses and the low hum of conversation, occasionally punctuated by a shot of high laughter.

He wondered if she was back at the party already. She didn't seem like the cautious type, running around in the dark after midnight while strange men chased after her. *Probably popped a few Advil and headed back to the dance floor*, he thought, scowling as he picked up the trowel and circled the bench where she'd been sitting. He imagined her swaying to the music, some new asshole with his hands on her waist, pressing her too damned close to his body.

A girl like that is trouble, he thought, *because every man who sees her wants her.*

Except me, he quickly amended. *I don't want you, Duchess. All I want is peace. And quiet.*

"*In other words, hold my hand.*" The words of the song popped into his head as he organized the empty plastic flats into a pile. "*In other words, baby, kiss me.*"

Kiss me.

He paused for a moment, one hand hovering distractedly over the tower of empty seedling flats, while he thought about Jacqueline Rousseau's offer of a kiss and how her cheeks had colored as he'd refused. Her meaning had been unmistakable, the luminous green orbs of her eyes nailing him from a few feet away, waiting for him, or daring him, to take her up on it.

His body had recognized the offer for exactly what it was, his blood sluicing with precision from his head to his dick, making it twitch and swell . . . which is exactly what had also forced him to drop her eyes. Make out with a girl who had a possible concussion? No. Absolutely not. No way.

It had taken a lot of willpower to turn her down, because God only knew where a kiss could have led, and his mind had been full of dirty fantasies since she'd shown up unannounced in the garden like a golden wood nymph, like a displaced duchess. But Gardener Thibodeaux wasn't in the habit of taking advantage of incapacitated women. Of *any* women, for that matter.

After a four-year career as a patrol officer and two years as a detective in the Special Victims Unit of the Philadelphia Police Department, he'd seen enough women taken advantage of—battered and bruised, and some left for dead—to last him a lifetime. If he lived to be a hundred and ten, he'd never consider making a move on a woman if there was even the slightest chance her wits were compromised, and the duchess, with that nasty gash on her head, might have regretted that kiss in the morning.

A quick vision of her luscious red lips flitted through his head, which annoyed him. *Stop thinking about her.*

He picked up the pile of flats and walked them to the area behind the gardener's cottage where Felix had instructed him to leave the empties until morning, when they could be taken to the dump. He opened the door of the nearby shed and put the trowel back on the magnetic strip over a wooden table that served as a workbench for plantings. He closed the door securely and locked it, walking the short distance from the shed to his apartment, mumbling the song lyrics ". . . *in other words, in other words . . . I love you . . .*" as *Fly Me to the Moon* came to its classic finale.

But despite his admonishment, he *couldn't* stop thinking about her as he drank his nightly cup of tea and straightened up the little apartment that he temporarily called home.

Was she hot?

Yes.

Was she intriguing, despite her brassy, sassy ways?

Yes.

Was she the most improbable fucking choice for—for—for *anything* having to do with him?

Oui, fucking *oui*.

He needed to forget about her curve-hugging gown, her perfect, highbrow Parisian French, and her stupid, sexy shoes. He needed to forget about her bright eyes and full lips, about the weight of her body in his arms and how it would feel beneath him. He needed to forget about the softness of her skin under the tips of his fingers and the way she said, "I believe you," as she stared up at him, wide-eyed and trusting.

He plunked his empty mug in the sink, showered, and toweled off, slipping between his sheets naked and staring up at the vague shadows dancing on the ceiling.

She was too young, too rich, too uppity, and *way* too much trouble for someone like Gardener, who was supposed to be rebuilding his life into a calm, safe, and stable place, none of which would be easily achieved with a distraction like Jacqueline Rousseau.

Forget about her.

It's for the best.

He closed his weary eyes and rolled to his side, facing the open window and letting another Frank Sinatra ballad lull him to sleep.

Chapter 3

Once Jean-Christian had seen her head and heard what had happened, he'd pledged to kill Tripp Stanton as soon as possible, but Jax had talked him off the ledge, asking him to please just escort her to her room, where she could take a couple of Advil and go to bed. She didn't want to waste any more brain power on Tripp.

Nor, she thought, as she lay her weary, aching head on her pillow, listening to the strains of *Fly Me to the Moon*, did she want to think about the gardener who'd simultaneously taken care of her and rejected her. Best intentions aside, however, she wasn't able to think about anything *but* the gardener as she stared at the ceiling, listening to the ambient noise of the party below.

There was something strange, almost mystical, about finding him working in the garden—the way he'd materialized out of shadows and moonlight, the stark contrast between his huge, masculine body and the delicate flowers he was planting so carefully.

Who was he? Someone the Englishes had hired to do some additional landscaping? Why was he an *ex*-cop? Where did he learn French, and why did she get the feeling that he was as comfortable speaking it as she, though he said he didn't speak it much anymore? He had raced to her aid, then carried her body in his arms across Westerly, through the hedges, and into Haverford Park to care for her injury. It was so romantic, it made her sigh. Or, at least, she'd *thought* it was romantic.

But obviously it wasn't to him. It was just an ex-cop's instinct. Nothing more.

She punched her pillow twice, huffing softly before lying back down on her uninjured side and closing her eyes.

Her mind played a pre–dream sequence of the night like a movie: her brother's storybook wedding to Kate, their beautiful reception under a tent with white twinkle lights and roses everywhere, the supertight security that had allowed Jax to actually enjoy herself until Tripp got annoying on the dance floor with his lewd, suggestive remarks . . . and then, running into the gardener and the moonlight garden. So ethereal. So unexpected. Followed, she grimaced, by her short confrontation with Tripp before she'd stumbled back and banged her head.

But opening her eyes to find herself being held by the gardener still felt like a sweet dream. *I wouldn't have saved you if my intention was to hurt you, Jacqueline*—his dark eyes and thick lashes. *I do, actually . . . I do have one to give*—and his smile . . . his smile . . . his beaut . . . ti . . . ful . . . sm . . .

She drifted off to sleep, listening to another Frank Sinatra ballad, and when she woke up the next morning, sunlight streamed into her bedroom, making her head throb like hell. She sighed and rolled over to look at the clock, her eyes widening when she realized that the bridal brunch, hosted by the English family at Haverford Park, was starting in thirty minutes, and she needed to get her ass in gear if she was going to make it.

"Good morning," called her twin sister, Madeleine, opening the door of Jax's bedroom as though she'd somehow known her sister had just woken up. Like most twins, they shared an inexplicable bond—a closeness that couldn't be quantified or explained and which Jax and Mad had pretty much always taken for granted.

"No, it's not," grumbled Jax, groaning as she sat up, making her head pound even worse.

Mad threw a bottle of Advil on the bed and put her hands on her hips. "J.C. told me what happened. How shall we kill him?"

Jax couldn't help grinning at her little sister, who was almost a full twenty minutes younger. In a pink flowered sundress with a matching powder-pink cardigan and her long dark hair back in a pink gingham hairband, Mad was a vision of innocence and loveliness. She wasn't killing anyone—unless it was with kindness—and they both knew it.

The Rousseau sisters had the same dark hair and green eyes, but that's where the similarities ended. They were fraternal twins who'd been blessed with very, very different personalities. Jax had always been the spitfire, the wild card, the sass, and her counterpart, Mad, was the sweet, the thoughtful, and—of all the Rousseau siblings—the most universally beloved.

"You? Hurt a fly?" Jax scoffed.

Mad sat down on the bed, placing a glass of water on her sister's bedside table and reaching up to gingerly touch the Band-Aid on Jax's temple.

"Bastard."

Jax opened the bottle and poured two pills into her hand. "*Oui.*"

"Are you going to press charges?"

Jax sighed, shaking her head. "And draw attention to myself? No, thanks."

Mad frowned. "So Tripp gets away with it."

Jax looked down at the pills miserably, then reached for the glass of water. "They'll splash it everywhere, Mad. Legal proceedings are public. It's not worth it."

"It makes me furious," said Mad softly.

"Join the club."

Mad sighed. "So . . . J.C. said that the Englishes' gardener came to your rescue."

Jax swallowed the pills before meeting her sister's eyes. "Something like that."

"But Felix was *here* all night . . . with Emily and Barrett English."

"New gardener."

"Ah-ha." Mad raised an eyebrow, somehow able to sense something distinct in her sister's otherwise truculent tone. "*Young* new gardener?"

Jax flushed. "Young-ish."

"*Hot* new gardener?" asked Mad, enjoying herself.

Jax scowled. "Hot-ish."

"So . . . ?"

"So what, Mad?" asked Jax, getting out of bed and stalking across her plush bedroom carpeting to the massive closet that held her clothes. "He's a gardener."

"Hold up. Hold up," said Mad from behind her. "What was *that*?"

Jax plucked a navy-blue silk tank top from a hanger and draped it over her arm, then turned and pulled some ivory-colored linen pants from the opposite side of the closet. "What do you mean?"

"You don't care what someone does for a living! You've dated bankers and actors, students, lawyers, horse groomers, that guy you met at Cannes who made the pretty lines in the beach sand every morning, the one from Vail who ran the ski lift, the Italian count who liked sucking on your—"

"Okay! You made your point. I date all kinds." Jax gave her sister a sour look as she threw the clothes on the bed. "But the neighbor's gardener? Can you imagine what *Maman* would say?"

"Since when do you give a shit?"

"Madeleine!"

"Jacqueline!" said Mad, mocking her.

Jax stared at her sister from across the bed, finally taking a deep breath and shrugging. "He wasn't interested."

Mad's eyes widened. "I must be going deaf because I'm sure you just said—"

"Don't make it worse," said Jax, looking down. "He wasn't—"

"Impossible," interrupted Mad, who crossed to her sister's bureau and took out a navy-blue push-up bra and white lace panties, which she handed to Jax. "They're *always* interested. You're . . . *you*."

"And apparently he's immune," said Jax, throwing her nightgown over her head and reaching for the bra.

"Again, I say . . . impossible."

Jax fastened the bra, then took the panties and stepped into them, pulling them up her long legs. "I made a pass at him."

"You what?" asked Mad, her eyes wide and surprised.

"I made a pass at him. I offered him a kiss and he . . . well, he didn't take me up on it," she said, buttoning the pants before zipping them. "Do you still have my navy Prada sandals? The patent-leather ones with the wedge?"

"I'll grab them for you in a minute," said Mad, still staring at her sister in awe. "You don't make passes. You don't need to. Ever."

"The fact that I haven't had much practice making the first move was more than obvious," said Jax acidly, shrugging into the whisper-soft silk top and heading for her bathroom.

After removing the velvet scrunchie, she brushed out her hair in front of the mirror. Checking her face, she noted some discoloration around the Band-Aid—lavender-and-yellow bruising—and Jax winced at the ugly swelling that spanned the space from her eye to her hairline. Damn Tripp anyway.

Suddenly Mad was beside her, dabbing concealer gently around the wound as she stared at her older sister in the mirror.

"*Chéri*," said Mad, avoiding Jax's eyes as she rubbed in the skin-colored liquid with a feather touch. "You need to be more careful. He could have really hurt you."

. . . *enroll yourself in a self-defense class if you're goin' to hang out with rapists* . . .

"I know," she said softly, shame coloring her cheeks.

"It must have been scary," said Mad, knowing it was true but also knowing how much it would bother Jax to admit it out loud.

Their eyes met in the mirror, and a moment of perfect twin-communication passed between them:

I hate this, thought Jax. *I hate feeling helpless.*

Mad nodded, her face concerned. *I know. I'm sorry.* She put the cap back on the makeup, put the container on the counter, and then pressed her lips to Jax's cheek. "*Je t'aime.*"

"I love you too."

"I think . . ." said Mad, her voice brightening as she grinned at Jax in the mirror. "I think you should go thank the hot, new gardener for his help. You'll feel better." She patted Jax on the shoulder. "I'll go find your sandals."

Jax watched her go in the mirror, applying some mascara and lipstick before pulling her long hair into a sleek ponytail at the nape of her neck.

A self-defense class.

Go thank the gardener.

She pulled her jewelry box from the corner cabinet and sat down at the vanity table, choosing three gold bangles and some oversized gold hoop earrings.

Go thank the gardener.

A self-defense class.

The ideas rolled around in her head as she finished getting ready and went downstairs, grabbing her sandals from where they dangled on Mad's fingers and following her sister out the front door to walk over to Haverford Park.

Gardener used to wake up at dawn, take a long jog around his South Philly neighborhood, shower, shave, dress, and head to work by eight, ready to take on the criminal element of Philadelphia and save the day. But since the accident and his forced retirement, he didn't have a good reason to wake up early anymore. Jogging outdoors wasn't an option with his compromised vision, and he couldn't exactly save the day by planting flowers and mulching rose gardens. Plus, the morning and early-afternoon light was almost unbearably bright for his eyes. So he really didn't wake up until after noon these days, and most of the time his day didn't really begin until three.

Part of him was grateful that he'd learned the nitty-gritty of gardening from his father, owner of the most sought-after landscaping company in New Orleans, where Gard was born and raised. Without a secondary skillset, he'd have been fucked, because his career as a detective had ended in the blink of an eye, no pun intended. Not that he really needed to work for the money. He had savings, plus his retirement pay was more than comfortable, especially since he'd been injured in the line of duty and been awarded a settlement in a civil case as well. But not working, he'd quickly learned, made him feel like shit, and since his chosen career path was now impossible, it was up to him to figure out an alternative. And while working as a temporary live-in gardener for a fancy house like Haverford Park wasn't where he'd envisioned his life at thirty-two years old, he also wasn't interested in running home to New Orleans, where his mama would take over his life with gusto. *Merci, non.*

He poured himself a cup of coffee and took it out on the tiny porch, resting one hand on the railing as he looked out over the hazy, fuzzy green of the estate lawn, which sprawled out in front of him and to his right. Nothing he saw had any definition. A watercolor-like puddle of blueish-white was the sky. Some undefined dark brown laying over the green could be tree trunks, he guessed. Something moved in the distance, and he cocked his head to the side and narrowed his eyes. Dark on top. Light on the bottom. Getting larger. Coming closer.

This was the part he hated the most. He knew it was a person, and by now, they could see him. They might be smiling at him. They might be frowning. Hell, they might be holding a gun. He didn't know. He'd *never* know. He was helpless without his eyes and he hated it. Turning to go inside, he stopped when he heard her voice.

"Gardener! Wait!"

He froze at her command.

Jacqueline Rousseau.

He'd recognize her voice till the day he died. His brain had already found a safe place for its keeping.

He turned slowly, bringing his cup to his lips, watching as the dark of her top and light of her pants got closer until he could make out the pink of her skin and the black of her hair. And finally, finally, those emerald-green eyes were only a foot or two away, and he could see them, almost clearly. And he sighed.

She stood before him, just across the railing from him, wearing a skimpy little navy-blue top with a bow in the

front and white pants molded to her long legs. Her hair
was back again today, but in a ponytail, not a chignon,
with a white bow tied low on the back of her neck. She
wasn't wearing deep-red lipstick as she had been last
night, but her lips . . . *merde*. Slick, pink, and pouty,
they were even more tempting today than they'd been
yesterday.

"Hi," she said.

"Mornin', Duchess."

"Morning?" She grinned. "It's almost three."

"I was up late helpin' damsels in distress," he said, feeling
foolish the moment the words left his lips.

She chuckled softly, however, making his risk pay off. "I
came to thank you."

"You're welcome."

She cocked her head to the side. "Do you have another
cup?"

He looked down at the mug in his hands. "Of coffee?"

"Yes. Thanks. I'd love some," she said cheekily.

He suspected she knew he hadn't really been offering,
but his mama hadn't raised a total cretin either. "Uh, sure.
Come on in."

He turned and headed back into the apartment, turning
right to go into the kitchen. He'd moved the bistro table
out of the center of the room almost as soon as he'd gotten
there, after banging into it twice. His peripheral vision just
wasn't what it used to be.

Taking a mug out of the cupboard over the stove, he set it
on the counter and poured her a cup of coffee.

"Milk?" he called. "Sugar?"

"Black," she answered, and he could tell from the placement of her voice that she'd taken a seat on the sofa where
he'd bandaged her head last night.

When he turned around, she was perched on its edge, looking up at him. He held out the mug to her from a safe distance. "Here you go."

"Thanks," she said, smiling again as she took a sip. "Mmm. It's good. What's in this?"

"It's chicory coffee," he said, taking another sip of his own.

"I've had this before . . . Hmm . . . oh! Ah-ha!" she exclaimed, placing her cup on the coffee table in front of her. "New Orleans! The coffee. Your accent. That's it. You're from New Orleans!"

"I am originally." He nodded. "You've been?"

"A couple of times. My brother, Étienne, went to law school there. Mad and I visited him a weekend or two."

"Mad?"

"Madeleine. My sister."

"Jax and Mad?" he asked, scowling at her for no good reason except that they had perfectly good names and used ridiculous nicknames instead. Gard had two sisters: Lily and Iris. Everyone called them Lily and Iris.

"That's us." She cleared her throat. "And *your* name is Gardener."

"I told you that last night. Several times."

"A gardener named Gardener? Surely you understand my confusion."

He stared at her, wondering why she was here, why she'd been asking about him, and who had told her his name, but before he could ask her, she'd already asked him another question.

"Why didn't you just say that Felix was thinking about retiring and you were trying out his job?"

He raised his cup and drank slowly, making her wait. "Why do you feel entitled to an explanation?"

She narrowed her eyes at him and offered primly, "It's absurd that a gardener should be named Gardener. You know that, don't you?"

Bossy, brassy, and a little rude when she didn't get her way, he decided. *Probably because beautiful girls with hot bodies get away with a lot.*

He stared at her for a moment, then shrugged. "If you say so, Duchess."

"I do."

He cut his eyes back to hers. "Anyone ever tell you that you come across as a snob?"

She raised an eyebrow in surprise, but her lips twitched like she thought he was funny. "Is your name really Gardener?"

"*Oui, Duchesse.*"

"And are you really the part-time gardener at Haverford Park?"

"For now. We'll see what happens."

"Then you do see . . . the irony."

"Not really," he said, shaking his head slowly, watching the way her tongue darted out to swipe her lips. His gaze lingered on her lips a touch too long, but he couldn't help it. It had been a while since he'd been with a woman, and this one was getting under his skin. He met her eyes. "Irony signals a difference between the appearance of things and reality. If anythin', my name is *un*ironic."

"I don't think your definition is right," she sniffed.

"I know it is."

"Are you a cop or a gardener or an English professor?"

"Don't get your panties in a wad," he drawled, smirking as he picked up his coffee and took a sip.

Why did all this feel like flirting? Or like foreplay? And why was he enjoying it so damn much? Much more than he should. He straightened his expression.

"A *wad*?" She wrinkled her nose, looking affronted. She shook her head and said under her breath, "A gardener named Gardener."

"A fact we've established," he said, giving her a bored look, though he didn't feel bored at all. "Repeatedly."

"How did that . . . *happen*?"

"The name or the job?"

"Both."

"Don't you have somewhere you need to be, Duchess?"

"And miss your scintillating explanation of this fascinating sobriquet-slash-profession collision? No way."

"My full name is Gardener Pierre Thibodeaux."

"Posh," she said.

He rolled his eyes at her, which only made her smile widen.

She cocked her head to the side. "Do you have a brother named Trowel? Or Rake?"

He shook his head. "Just two sisters."

"Named?"

His mother would have laughed and told him he was about to "walk into the poo." He sighed. "Lily and Iris."

"Ha!" she said, her eyes bright with delight. "Flowers! You're messing with me!"

He shook his head, forfeiting a smile to her because she was just that adorable and it was almost impossible not to enjoy her. "Nope. My father was a landscaper. I guess he thought . . ."

"He'd mix business and pleasure?"

"Something like that."

"Well, it's good to meet you, Gardener Thibodeaux."

He watched her as she said this, taking a ridiculous amount of pleasure in the way she said his name and wanting to hear her say it again and again.

"It's good to meet *you*, Duchess."

They weren't touching. He was sitting across from her in a chair, a coffee table and two steaming mugs of chicory coffee between them, and yet he felt a zap of electricity shoot through his body as surely as if they'd both been shocked with a live wire. She must have felt it too because her cheeks colored.

She cleared her throat, dropping her eyes to her coffee mug. "We've established Gardener the name. Now, how about gardener the job?"

"I was a cop," he said.

"Here in Philly?"

He nodded.

"Why not in New Orleans?"

"Change of scenery."

She narrowed her eyes. "I bet there's a story there."

There was, but he didn't feel like sharing it with her.

He didn't answer, so she plowed forth. "Why aren't you a cop anymore? Why work here at Haverford Park?"

"You ask a lot of questions."

"Is that a problem?"

He took a deep breath and let it go slowly. Maybe it was. How much did he want her in his business? For that matter, why was she still here? She'd said thank-you. It's not like they were going to be friends or something. So what was her game?

He met her eyes and held them for a long moment before asking, "What do you want, *Jacqueline*?"

She leaned away from him. "I wanted to say thank-you."

"You're welcome," he said, standing up and glancing meaningfully at the door.

It was fucking with his head, sitting here chatting with her over coffee. The more time he spent with her, the more time he wanted with her, but he'd already determined her an unlikely candidate for a friend and a disastrous choice for anything more, no matter how much his dick disagreed. He saw her coming from a mile away with her designer clothes, entitled manners, and pushy questions. He was trying to build a quiet, new life for himself, and he didn't need the distraction of Jacqueline Rousseau.

He needed her to go.

As though she knew she was about to get the boot, she said, "I wanted to ask a favor."

"A favor?"

She nodded, looking up at him from where she still sat on his couch. "Weston English said that you used to work in the Special Victims Unit."

Shit. Weston was talking about him? Was he also gossiping about the accident? Fuck. Gard wasn't interested in his business being discussed by virtual strangers. He didn't want her to—well, if she knew what had happened, she'd look at him differently, wouldn't she? Yes. Of course she would. And why that mattered he wasn't certain, but it did. It mattered to him that Jax Rousseau *never* looked at him with sympathy or pity.

"What else did he say?" he asked roughly, feeling pissed.

She shrugged. "Not much. He was surprised when you applied for this job. Said you used to be a detective for the SVU before retiring. Said you helped him out with a couple of cases he worked on at the DA's office. And he said you were a really, really great cop."

Something inside of him twisted at her words. Not because she meant to hurt him, but because he *had* been a good cop, and he had *loved* his job. He searched her face, looking for signs of pity, but he didn't see any. "So . . . ?"

"So last night you told me I should take a self-defense class if I plan to hang around rapists."

He raised his eyebrow, giving her a dry, impatient look.

"And since most of the guys I know are . . . well, like Tripp, you know, when they drink . . . well, I was thinking that maybe you're right. It couldn't hurt to take a few classes . . . so . . ."

Something about her tone made him anxious. "So take a class."

She shook her head. "Nope. I want you."

I want you.

His brain short-circuited for a moment. His skin flushed hot. His dick jumped behind his sweat pants, every fast beat of his heart making it throb.

"*Wh-what*?"

"I want *you* . . . you know, to teach me."

"Teach you *what*?" he asked in a rush.

"How to defend myself," she said, her forehead wrinkling in annoyance. "What have I been saying?"

You've been saying "I want you," which is something you should never say to a man unless you mean it in the only way that matters.

Gard rotated his neck from side to side, listening to it crack as he took a beat to catch his breath and try to focus on what she was saying, not on the dirty fantasies lapping through his head.

Self-defense. Wait. Self-defense classes?

"I don't teach self-defense classes."

"Oh, really?" She stood up, giving him a sour look. "You have no idea how to defend yourself?"

"Of course I do. But I'm not a teache—"

"If you know how, you can teach me."

"Go to your local YMCA. They must have a class."

She opened her mouth, then closed it, her whole body seeming to deflate before him. When she finally spoke, her voice wasn't as strong or sassy as it had been a moment before. "I can't."

"Why not? Too good to take a class with the unwashed masses?"

She grimaced, drawing back as she would if he'd slapped her. "No. That's not it at all."

"Then what?"

"I'm . . ."

"You're what?"

She took a deep breath. "They'll take pictures."

"Who?"

"They'll . . . I mean, they . . . forget it." Her voice was soft and tired as she dropped his eyes. "I should go."

"Wait jus—"

"Thanks for the coffee."

He blew out a frustrated breath, hating the conflicted way he felt as he watched her sidestep between the coffee table and sofa, her head down as she neared the door.

"Jax," he said gently but firmly, drawing his fingers into fists by his sides. She stopped. "*Who* will take pictures?"

"Everyone," she said softly, turning to face him with glassy eyes. "I won an Oscar last year for producing *The Philly Story*. My last name is Rousseau. Suddenly I was linked to every actor and director in Hollywood. They sneaked into my gym and tried to get pictures of me coming out of the shower. Another one chased me on his motorcycle until I rear-ended another car. Thank God no one was seriously hurt." Her eyes flooded with tears, and she reached up to brush the Band-Aid still affixed to her temple. "It'll be all over Instagram and Twitter: *Jax Rousseau with a black eye. Jax Rousseau taking a self-defense class. Who beat up Jax Rousseau?* They'll make up stories and say things. It'll start all over again and I can't . . ." She shook her head, one hand swiping away the wetness on her cheeks. "Forget it. Not your problem. I'll find someone else."

His chest clenched, watching her get emotional over the possibility of professional gossipmongers invading her privacy, and he knew instinctively it was why she'd been so standoffish last night. And damn it but it made him angry. It made him furious. It made him desperate to protect her, even though he couldn't—even though he was a shadow of the man he once was.

"I'll do it," he blurted out, releasing his breath as his lungs relaxed. "I'll teach you."

She was halfway out the door, but she whipped around to face him, her face brightening, her chin lifting. "You will?"

He nodded. "Yeah."

"I'll pay you."

He didn't like her offering him money. Couldn't put his finger on why, because she *should* pay him for his time, but he hated the thought of taking her money. "We'll discuss that later. Where should we meet?"

"Uhhh . . . Le Chateau? We have a gym."

"Of course you do." He paused. "You live there? With your parents?"

"My mother was just in town for the wedding. She returns to Paris tomorrow."

He sensed there was more to her explanation and couldn't deny he was curious, but it was none of his business. "Shouldn't take more than three lessons to teach you a few important moves. Three o'clock tomorrow work for you, Duchess?"

She smiled at him, and glory Lord, he knew he was in trouble, because when this woman looked happy, she was so fucking stunning that something inside of him wanted to make her happy every minute of every day, just so he could take some credit for that much beauty.

"Tomorrow," she said, opening the door and stepping through before glancing at him over her shoulder one last time. Her emerald eyes sparkled. His heart leapt. "It's a date."

A date.

Merde.

Chapter 4

Jax's mother, Liliane, kissed her on both cheeks before cupping her daughter's face and smiling at her. "Come and see me soon, *chéri*? *Avec Madeleine*?"

Jax nodded. "*Oui, Maman*. We'll come in August or September."

"Call me when you return to Hollywood. Once you're settled."

"I will," she said, stepping away from her mother's touch. She had no idea if or when she might return to California, but her mother didn't want to hear that. Her mother liked having an Oscar-winning, Hollywood producer for a daughter.

Liliane looked at the Mediterranean-style mansion behind her daughter and sniffed. "I never liked this place, you know. And the way the previous owners called it *Chateau Nouvelle*. Tsk. You father thought it was . . . *amusing*."

"You've had it officially changed to Le Chateau now."

Her mother waved a perfectly manicured hand dismissively. "*C'est trop tard*." *It's too late*.

Jax looked back at the house that she loved so much, that had always felt like home more than any other place on earth.

"I should sell it," said Liliane, looking up at the house with a frown.

Jax curled her fingers into her palm. "Really? Now?"

"*Oui.*" Liliane shrugged. "Eventually."

Carefully controlling her voice to sound sympathetic and cajoling, Jax placed an arm around her mother's thin shoulders and led her down the grand steps to the town car waiting in the driveway to take her to the airport.

"Such chaos, *chère Maman*. The expense of realtors and movers. The inconvenience. Dissolving an estate? After all the work you put into Étienne's wedding? What a nightmare." She shuddered dramatically for effect, then stopped beside the car as the chauffeur quickly hopped out of the driver's seat to open the back door for Liliane. "If anything, you deserve a rest."

Jax's mother sighed, then nodded as she pulled her daughter into her arms for one final embrace. "You are right. Now is not the time."

"*Oui,*" murmured Jax, her sense of reprieve so sharp, it almost made her light-headed. "*Au revoir, Maman.*"

"*Au revoir, chéri.*"

In one elegant move that recalled her mother's one-time profession as a ballerina, Liliane Rousseau slid into the waiting car and the driver shut the door. Jax took a step back, pulling her Tiffany-blue pashmina tighter around her body as she lifted a hand to wave good-bye.

As the car disappeared down the driveway and through the gates of Le Chateau, onto Blueberry Lane, Jax slumped with relief.

"What was that all about?" asked Mad from the top step, a rolling suitcase just behind her.

"She was talking about selling the house. Again."

"I swear, she knows how much it bothers you," said Mad, her lips thin, her green eyes angry.

Jax walked up the steps between them. "You're going too?"

"Mm-hm. Thatcher's coming home tonight. I thought I'd make him dinner."

Thatcher was Mad's longtime boyfriend, whom Mad kept expecting to pop the question, but there was no popping in sight, unless you counted all the times Dr. Thatcher Worthington popped out of town to attend medical conferences.

"Don't look at me like that," said Mad. "He works hard."

"It was Étienne's wedding, Mad. I think he could have skipped *one* conference to escort you."

"He's one of the leading clinical psychiatrists in the country, Jax. He can't just—" Mad used air quotes. "—'skip a conference' anytime he feels like it."

"I'd just like to see him putting you first," said Jax, reaching out to push a long strand of jet-black hair behind her sister's shoulder.

"He *does*. Don't worry about me and Thatcher. We're practically a done deal, big sister." She waggled her bare ring finger and grinned at Jax. "And listen, J.C. asked for a ride, but he's still sleeping, so he's on his own. If he's too hungover, call him a cab when he finally wakes up, huh?"

"No problem. Sure you don't want to stay for another couple of hours? We could have lunch."

"Rain check? I had this idea: a new program I could offer the kids, and I wanted to spend a little time working on a plan to present to Harvey."

Madeleine Rousseau worked as a librarian in the Children's Department of the Philadelphia Free Library, and she was always trying to come up with new and innovative programs to offer to the children of Philadelphia.

"What is it this time?" asked Jax. "And how can I help?"

"Music and Movement was such a success for the toddlers . . . I was thinking we should offer a similar class to grade-school kids after school this fall. It could even be a drop-off. Public schools keep cutting the arts, and I just . . ." Mad grinned. "I'm on my soapbox again."

"But you look so gorgeous standing up there," teased Jax.

Mad rolled her eyes. "I need to do some research, figure out the costs, find someone to lead it . . ."

"You know you're just going to end up paying for it again."

"I will if I have to." Mad shrugged. "I have millions, Jax."

It was true. They all had millions. All four Rousseau children had trust funds that amounted to approximately twenty-five million dollars apiece, and three of the four siblings augmented it in their own way—Étienne and J.C. with their company, The Rousseau Trust, and Jax with a recent movie she'd produced to great acclaim. Mad was the exception. She was far better at giving her money away.

"You're going to go bankrupt someday," said Jax, hooking her arm through her sister's and walking her down the stairs to a cute red BMW convertible.

"Then I'll rush to my rich sister and beg her to take me in."

Jax grinned at Mad with love. "She will, you know. She *always* will."

"I know," said Mad, stopping by her car and leaning forward to kiss Jax on the cheek. "How's the eye?"

Jax shrugged. It ached less today, but the bruising looked worse.

"Jax, now that you're back, why don't you think about getting a place in the city? We could find a co-op with great security. We could—"

"No," she said, her voice clipped and final. "I prefer it here."

Becoming a movie producer had changed Jax's entire life, and not, unfortunately, in a good way.

She'd grown up with magazines like *Philadelphia Today* and *Town & Country* taking pictures of her and her family, of course, and had become accustomed to seeing her picture in the newspaper society pages from time to time. But she hadn't been prepared for the sort of exposure that producing a movie or winning an Academy Award would generate. Suddenly, she couldn't leave her Beverly Hills apartment without gossip rags and entertainment magazines taking an interest in her too, and it was a different kind of paparazzi than the gentle, respectful kind she'd been used to back in Philly.

They waited for her outside of the studio, their cameras clicking, shooting rapid-fire questions at her about her love life, sex life, and future movies as she drove from the safety of the electric gates onto the street. They took pictures of her coming out of the grocery store and harassed her friends for information about her. In *Star Tracks* and *Listen Up!* they commented on her hair and clothes, speculated about her love interests, and made up stories about her life. If she wasn't smiling, she was bitchy. If she looked thin, she was anorexic. If she bought ice cream, she was depressed. If she was talking to a man, she was getting engaged . . . or dumped. Every word she said on Facebook or Twitter had been analyzed and dissected—until she'd stopped posting altogether and closed her accounts.

Overnight she'd lost her privacy and had only been able to reclaim it by packing up her things, selling her apartment in California, and returning to the safety of Le Chateau, where she'd found solace and protection in its exclusive neighborhood setting, high gates, and state-of-the-art security system.

Jax looked over her shoulder at the yellow-colored stone mansion with thirty shiny windows and a set of three elegant French doors at the grand entrance that looked out over the circular drive where the sisters stood together. It was an ostentatious house. Yes. And she remembered her father chuckling with delight at the ludicrous, grammatically incorrect French name bestowed upon it by the previous owners. But it was her home, and for two months, ever since she'd moved home in April, it was the only place where Jax truly felt comfortable. This enormous pile of stone on Blueberry Lane was her safe haven, and she loved it with all her heart.

"No," she said again, gentler than before. "I'm happy here."

"Will you produce another movie?" asked Mad, her voice tentative.

"Now that the wedding's over, I can look through the stack of scripts in my room," Jax answered, hedging the question with forced levity as Mad unlinked their arms, collapsed the handle of her suitcase, and lifted it into her trunk.

Jax didn't fool her sister. Mad's face was still troubled.

"Jax, truth?"

"If you insist."

"You're hiding here. Avoiding life. Maybe even a little stuck."

"So what if I am? Is that a crime?"

"No. But I'm worried about you."

"My privacy was totally invaded. Shredded. I was practically hunted. It was awful to feel like someone's prey, to be constantly looking over my shoulder and having no legal recourse."

"I can't believe that lawyer wouldn't press charges when you got into the accident."

"He couldn't!" exclaimed Jax, her frustration and anger rising. "The photographer had a helmet on that hid his face. And I didn't get a look at the tiny license plate on the back of his motorcycle. He sped away before I could see it. Mad, I could've killed that woman I hit! I could've really hurt her or someone else."

"It wasn't your fault," said Mad, reaching for her sister.

"Doesn't matter," said Jax, pulling away. "Just, please, try to understand: I feel safe here. I don't want to live in the city."

"I *do* understand." Mad sighed, reaching out to place a gentle hand on her sister's arm. "But it's been months. What's next for you?"

Jax didn't have an answer. She pursed her lips, part of her wishing she had a ready answer, the other part wishing Mad would get going and stop asking her questions that felt so daunting.

"You need to rebound at some point." Mad tilted her head to the side, searching her twin's face. "It's okay to take a little while to figure out what comes next, Jax . . . as long as it doesn't take forever."

"We can't all graduate from college and nab our dream job out of the gate," said Jax, her voice edgy, her lips pursed.

Mad gave her a look. "I was stacking books for three years before they offered me assistant librarian, and even then, it wasn't in the Children's Department. Didn't matter what my last name was, and you know it. I had to *earn* my job there."

"I know. I know. I just meant . . . you always knew what you wanted to do. Me? Not so much."

After college, Jax had bought a share in a horse breeding farm outside of Philadelphia that had turned out to be a bad investment. Feeling duped and furious about her lack of legal recourse, she'd enrolled in law school at the University of Pennsylvania, where she'd attended classes for two years but never completed her degree. While on campus one afternoon, she'd run into a sorority sister who'd told Jax she was producing a movie, and with her friend's help and connections, Jax had put together and financed her own project, *The Philly Story*, a remake of the 1940 classic *The Philadelphia Story*, and moved out to California to follow the postproduction process. It was an Oscar darling, and she'd taken home the gold statue.

And that's when the nightmare had started—paparazzi hounding her every move. She took a deep breath and sighed as Mad slammed the trunk of her car and took her keys out of her purse.

"I'm only twenty-seven," said Jax, following her sister as she rounded the car and opened the driver's door. "I don't have to decide my whole life today, Mad."

"That's true," said Mad. "And there's nothing wrong with taking a break. But don't hide away here forever, huh?" She looked up at the enormous façade of Le Chateau. "It's too big a house for one small girl."

No, it's not. It's my home and I love it.

Jax let her sister pull her into a warm embrace. Mad grinned at her as she drew away. "Come for dinner on Thursday?"

"I wouldn't miss it," said Jax, watching as Mad slipped into her seat with the same effortless grace as their mother.

"Am I invited?" yelled J.C., who appeared suddenly behind Jax, running toward their sister's car with a wild case of bed-head, a bare chest, and unbuttoned jeans.

"Yes," said Mad, giving him a saucy look. "You almost missed your ride back to Philly, sleepyhead."

J.C. gave Jax a quick kiss on the cheek as he threw his duffel bag into the backseat of Mad's car and jumped into the passenger seat beside her. He pulled on some sunglasses and grinned at his baby sister. "Ready, Jeeves."

Jax chuckled at their antics, waving as Mad pulled away.

Finally she turned and walked backed back to the house. All their relatives and family friends had left yesterday, and Étienne and Kate wouldn't be returning from their honeymoon in romantic Mooréa for three weeks. Everyone was gone.

Aside from the skeleton staff—a part-time cook hired by Jax, in addition to her mother's housekeeper, Mrs. Jefferson, two part-time maids, and a gardener/groundskeeper—Jax was now alone. And after the mad rush of the last two weeks, when the estate was full of guests and aflutter with wedding plans, it felt lonesome and welcome all at the same time.

She closed one of the three front doors behind her and ducked into a front room to the right of the entryway—a masculine man cave that had once been her father's study—and sat down at the desk. Clicking on the mouse, she pulled up the security system feeds and made sure the front gates closed and locked after Mad pulled through them. They didn't have fences between Le Chateau and the abutting estates—Westerly, owned by the Winslows, and Forrester, owned by the Storys. There had never been a need, and Jax prayed there never would be. She liked the freedom of roaming around the neighborhood on a beautiful afternoon—checking out the Winslows' famous gardens or sitting beside the pond at Forrester—and knowing that she was safe from prying eyes behind the secure gates of her neighbor's homes.

Plus, she thought, a catlike grin spreading across her lips, in about two hours, a certain gardener would be walking across Westerly's lawn to meet her, and she liked the idea of him making his way to her discreetly. Discretion had become paramount in her life.

Especially when hot men were in play.

Even, she thought, frowning, *when they appeared to have zero interest in her.*

Satisfied that Le Chateau was secure, she minimized the window on the computer screen and headed upstairs to get changed for her lesson. While the idea of a self-defense class probably wouldn't have occurred to Jax on her own, something about the idea greatly appealed to her once Gardener had made the suggestion. Over the last four or five months, she'd lost so much control over her life. Learning to defend herself physically felt like a strong step toward reclaiming her self-reliance.

As she climbed the grand staircase to her bedroom, she toyed with the idea of wearing her skimpiest, sexiest workout clothes. Would he notice? Probably. Would he care? Probably not.

"Quit thinking about him," she said aloud, feeling annoyed. *You're not taking a class to see him.* Taking lessons was something she was doing for herself—to learn how to protect herself and start building up her strength and confidence again. Right? Of course, right.

Plus, she thought pragmatically, groaning at the growing stack of scripts beside her desk as she stepped into her bedroom, it was a welcome distraction from her life. It would make her feel productive to learn a new skill, even if she was technically "stuck," as Mad had observed.

And as far as distractions went, her instructor, despite his rude and gruff ways, and especially when he smiled, wasn't too shabby.

The walk from Haverford Park to Le Chateau probably took most people about ten minutes if they walked across the lawns and through gates and hedges at a brisk clip, but Gardener knew it could take him up to twenty minutes, since he'd be walking slowly, careful not to bump into anything, lacking the long-distance and peripheral vision to make the journey efficient, but taken for granted by everyone else.

Uncertain of what equipment the duchess would have at her "gym," he threw some dumbbells, a blow-up punching bag, and a towel into a duffel bag and tossed it over his shoulder. Then he grabbed his collapsible walking stick, locked his apartment door, and set forth.

He'd walked over to Westerly twice before—once with Felix to meet the gardener of the adjoining property and once on his own to ask to borrow a double-male connector for the hose when he'd inadvertently stepped on theirs and broken it. He knew where the patio was and how to get around it. He walked confidently over the bright-green grass, taking his time when he saw a blur of brown (tree trunks) or gray (stone benches, large, landscaped boulders, or small outbuildings) in the distance and trying to remember its placement as he grew close enough to identify what it was. Finally, met with a five-foot-high wall-like structure of varying shades of green before him, he knew he'd reached the hedgerow that separated Westerly from Le Chateau. Looking up over the chin-high shrubbery, he could make out the yellowish stone of the adjoining estate mansion some distance away. The only problem? The hedgerow itself.

Hedgerows were, quite literally, rows of tangled hedges, sometimes four or five feet deep. Almost impossible to walk through, unless you were a squirrel or rabbit, they were a great choice for impassable natural beauty when property owners didn't feel like opting for fences. Because the Rousseaus and Winslows were, as far as Gardener could tell, friendly neighbors and because Jax had obviously walked from Le Chateau to Westerly on Saturday night, there had to be a break in the hedgerow with an opening or gate. If he could find it, he could get through.

Raising his wrist to a few inches beneath his eyes, he looked at the time. Two fifty-five. Shit. This walk had taken a little longer than he thought. He looked up, hoping for an opening to magically appear, but the messy green blur of the barrier looked solid both right and left as far as his eyes could see.

"Fuck," he muttered, starting to the left.

The thing that really frustrated Gard was that for anyone with halfway normal vision, the entrance would be clear. It was *right here* somewhere. And yet for him, it was elusive. It wasn't fair. It wasn't fucking fair, and it pissed him off to have been robbed of his independence, of his God-given right to *see*.

He poked his stick into the row and started running alongside it, hoping that he'd find the void and wouldn't trip, but he got to the end of the row before realizing that left had been the wrong choice. Turning around as he murmured a string of curses, he switched his stick to the other hand and ran back down the row, jogging past the void, though luckily his stick pattered on the slats of a picket fence, telling him to back up.

Sweating and panting, he took several steps back and there it was: the cutout in the hedge with a little white gate almost hidden between the rows. Walking quickly through and fastening the gate behind him, he trudged across the green lawn toward the massive yellow structure, then bore to the left, able to make out the shape and color of a circular gravel driveway. Pausing by the corner of the house, he folded up his stick and tucked it into the duffel, then swiped his forearm over his sweaty face.

Forcing himself to walk in a way that looked leisurely, not frazzled, he made his way around the building, staring at the ground so he wouldn't stumble. He stopped when he came to a set of stairs and ascended five steps that—presumably— led to the main entrance of the house.

Standing before the door, he looked for a bell, but finding none, he knocked and waited.

And waited.

Hmm. Nothing.

No sound of footsteps. No hot brunette. Nobody.

He knocked again, then pressed his ear to the window, hoping to hear the sound of her making her way to the door. Still nothing.

How late was he anyway? He held up his watch close to his eyes again. Three twelve. Shit. Did she think he'd stood her up? While he didn't love the idea of teaching her, he wouldn't want her to think he'd just flake out without a word either.

He knocked again, more forcefully this time, his frustration about the walk and the hedgerow and his general resentment about his lot in life making the knock sound more like a bang.

"Coming! Coming!"

His heart.

Oh Lord, his fucking heart nearly beat out of his goddamned chest at the sound of her voice.

He stood back from the door, wiping the relieved smile off his face and steeling his expression.

The door opened.

He smelled her before he saw her, before she came into focus, and it took all of his fucking willpower not to close his eyes and breathe her in like oxygen. Much like his ears had sharpened over the past year, Gard's sense of smell had sharpened too. Combined with a lifelong working knowledge of plants and herbs, it wasn't hard to sort through the mix of scent that was Jax: rosemary . . . and lemons.

Fucking heaven.

"Hi!" she said, holding the door open.

"Hi," he said, walking through it.

He looked around, expecting to find himself in a grand entry hall, but they were in a small study-like room instead.

He breathed in, wrinkling his nose as he traded Jax's fresh scent for old cigars and leather.

"Why'd you come to the side door?" asked Jax. "It's a wonder I even heard you. The study door was closed."

Fuck. He'd gone to the wrong door. Must have been one of those houses with all sorts of doors along the front façade.

He cleared his throat, following her through the study and into the grand entry hall he'd been originally expecting.

"Just went to the first door I found, Duchess. When there are fifty, it's hard to choose the right one."

She turned to face him. "Well, anyway . . . you're here."

Close enough to touch, and therefore close enough to see clearly, he let his eyes linger on the loveliness of her face for a long moment before dropping them . . . and the next breath he sucked in had nothing to do with cigars or rosemary. On her mouthwatering little body she wore a bright-aqua sports bra and skintight black nylon leggings that just made it to her knees. Her flat stomach was bare. Her legs and feet were bare. As he stared at her feet, he exhaled slowly, running his eyes back up her body, checking out her legs, the slight flare of her hips, her tight waist, tan stomach, and full, perky breasts. Since it was impossible not to ogle, he didn't attempt to conceal it, slowly making his way back to her eyes to find them sparkling with amusement.

"Do I pass inspection?" she asked, smiling at him.

He scowled at her, taking a deep breath. Had she done this for his benefit? His dick thanked her for her thoughtfulness. The rest of him was slightly pissed off about the distraction. He was here to teach her how to defend herself, not make himself so sexually frustrated that he'd be up half the night jacking off to relieve his lust.

"Where's the gym?"

Her smile faded just a touch as she arched an eyebrow at him. "Downstairs."

"Lead the way. I've only got an hour."

"I wouldn't want to keep you," she said, her voice losing its warmth.

He'd hurt her feelings, and that really hadn't been his intention, but all things considered, it was probably for the best. The more he could keep a little distance between them, the better it would be for both of them.

Trudging downstairs, he couldn't help but check out her ass, a thing of incredible beauty in second-skin Lycra. She was in good shape. She shouldn't need more than a few lessons before he'd feel like she could at least get herself out of a bad situation. And that was the point, right? Not to spend time with her. Just to make sure she could protect herself from future assholes.

"So . . . you're involved with movies?"

She turned right at the bottom of the stairs. "Yep."

"You live out in LA?" he asked.

"I'm staying here for a while."

"I was wonderin' . . ." he started.

"About what?"

"You mentioned people taking pictures of you."

She stiffened. "Mm-hm."

"Did you really win an Oscar?"

"My movie did," she answered.

They were in a long cream-colored hallway with recessed lighting and classy framed black-and-white pictures on the wall. He passed a room on the right that read "Screening" on the dark-glass door and another across the hall that read "Studio."

"Are you an actress?"

"Nope. Producer."

"Are producers generally bothered by the paparazzi?"

To his left, they passed three clear-glass sliding doors leading to what he assumed to be a pool from the rectangular-shaped aqua blob surrounded by what appeared to be gray slate.

"I don't know," she said. "Maybe they are. If they're only twenty-seven and . . ."

Smokin' hot.

"And . . . ?"

"Their family's already, you know, on the media's radar."

"Like Paris Hilton?"

She turned around to face him, stopping before another dark-glass door that read "Gym/Spa."

"No," she said emphatically, her green eyes wide and angry. "*Not* like Paris."

Gard stopped walking, standing before her, close enough that her unusual combination of lemons and rosemary made his senses soar a little. Her glower brought him back to earth.

"I'm *nothing* like Paris. I didn't *ask* for that attention! I didn't go on TV and open up my life to speculation by starring in a reality show! I never made a sex tape that was—" she put her fingers over her lips in an exaggerated gesture of surprise "—oops! leaked onto the Internet." She took a deep breath and let it out through her nose in a huff. "I love movies. I just wanted to produce one. Did you know it was filmed here? On location? I just wanted to remake my favorite movie, to see Le Chateau on the big screen. I didn't know I'd lose every ounce of privacy, that I'd be stalked like an animal—"

Her eyes filled with tears and she stopped abruptly, lowering her eyes and swallowing. And suddenly, she didn't look like a duchess or a femme fatale or even the heiress that she was. She looked like a girl who felt lost and alone . . . and his heart ached for her because Gard understood lost and he understood alone. He'd lived equal parts lost and alone every day of his life since the accident.

Reaching out, he slipped his fingers under her chin and raised it gently until she met his gaze. She was so beautiful, her expression so vulnerable and naked, his breath caught and he held it, his lungs burning as she stared back at him, her misery betrayed in the tremble of her lips and the glisten in her eyes.

"First rule of self-defense . . ."

Near his fingers, the pulse in her throat leapt wildly, matching the fierce beating of his heart. Regardless of the intimacy that seemed to grow like a warm, living thing between them . . . regardless of the slippery slope that was his unwanted attraction for this virtual stranger . . . and regardless of the imminent danger of slipping, of sliding, of falling into whatever ill-advised chasm lay between them, he held her eyes captive with his.

"First rule, *Jacqueline*," he repeated softly, his throat dry, his voice husky. "No matter what . . . don't ever look away."

Chapter 5

It was jarring and intimate to hold eye contact for so long, but Jax dug deep inside for the strength not to look away.

As the seconds ticked by, locked in his gaze, it surprised her to feel something galvanize within her. Broken pieces of something shattered started pulling back together as though they were fitted with magnets, like lost puzzle pieces seeking out their scattered mates, wanting to be whole again. It made her feel different—excited or energetic or hopeful, somehow—and after several months of feeling disillusioned, different felt . . . well, *good*.

After staring at each other for a solid minute without speaking, she somehow managed to compose herself and open the door to the gym, turning away from him and into the mirror-walled workout room. Gardener, who stood in the doorway behind her, whistled low, taking in the space, which housed an elliptical machine, a stationary bike, a treadmill, a punching bag hanging from the ceiling, a ballet bar, a full rack of dumbbells, two benches, and a home gym with arm, chest, and back press functions. In the far-left corner of the room was a door that led to a sauna, and a door in the far-right corner led to a bathroom, complete with a rainforest shower and Jacuzzi tub.

"You weren't kiddin' when you said you had a gym," he said.

She tossed him a look over her shoulder. "You assumed I was?"

He squinted as he looked around the room. "Duchess, the only *home gyms* I've ever seen lately had a stationary bike stuck in a basement . . . maybe with a crappy black-and-white TV on a table nearby. This is . . ."

From a cabinet just inside the door, she plucked a remote control and pressed a button that made a bracket in the ceiling open. A small television set descended to the perfect viewing height in front of the stationary bike.

"*Voila*," she said. "Bike and TV."

From behind her, he chuckled softly, and it made her smile, but she didn't look at him, because instinct told her that if she did, he'd stop laughing and frown at her, and she liked the sound of his laugher way too much to imperil it. She savored the brief sound, finally turning to face him when he was silent again.

"Well? Shall we get started?"

His squinting eyes, still searching the room, cut to her face and focused. "Yeah. Okay." He shrugged his shoulder and the duffel bag he was carrying slid down his arm. He caught the strap and lowered the bag the rest of the way to the ground.

"What's in there?"

"Stuff we don't need."

"Why not?"

"Because you've got everythin' I need right here."

She knew that he was talking about gym equipment. She knew that. But she couldn't seem to keep herself from taking his words out of context for just a moment and trying them out in a different way in her head:

. . . you've got everything I need right here.

"Oh, *merde*," she whispered, sighing softly.

"Duchess?" he prompted.

"Hmm?" she asked, snapping her head up to look at him. She plastered a smile on her face and pushed her ponytail off her shoulder. "Yes. I'm ready. Let's get to it!"

He nodded, taking a deep breath and nailing her with a hard glare. "I'm going to teach you about the eyes today. Yours first, then your assailant's. Now . . . what's the first rule?"

"Don't ever look away."

"Right. Why not?"

He had his feet spread apart and his hands on his hips. His sweat pants were a little big, but his plain white T-shirt was a little snug, fitting over his chest like a glove and high-lighting the ridiculously defined ridges of muscle.

Umm, she thought, *we don't look away because what we see is so hot?*

"*Jacqueline?*"

And the way he said her name . . . it turned her insides to warm honey. She hid a whimper by clearing her throat. "Because . . ."

"Because awareness is the first rule of avoidance. And avoidance is the name of the game."

She nodded. "Okay."

"You understand what I mean?"

"I assume you mean that if you don't put yourself into dangerous situations, you won't need to defend yourself."

"Exactly," he said, crossing his arms over his chest. "No checkin' out Facebook on your phone in a parkin' lot. No wearin' headphones unless you're safe at home in your bed. Make eye contact to show you're unafraid. Be aware of your surroundin's. Anyone who's within three feet of your person is too close."

"Three feet," she said, nodding.

"Do you know how much that is?" he asked, uncrossing his arms.

"From you to me?"

"No. We're five feet away from each other." He took a step toward her. "Now we're three feet apart. Extend your arm." She did as he asked, her fingertips brushing his chest. "Your arm is approximately three feet long. Does that help you gauge things?"

"I can't go around with my arms spread wide all the time."

"Of course not. But look at me. Look at my eyes. Look how far apart we are. Remember this distance."

She looked into his eyes—*again*—but she was slightly more relaxed this time and paid closer attention. *How funny*, she thought. *They're asymmetrical, one slightly higher than the other.* Stepping forward—approximately two feet from his person, which was, by his own definition, too close—she further noted that there was scar tissue on his face that she hadn't noticed before. It looked like he'd had extremely bad acne concentrated around his eyes or had picked a bunch of chicken pox sores that had left small craters around his eyes and on his forehead, though something intuitive told her that neither of those reasons was right.

"What happened?" she whispered, still staring deeply into his dark-brown eyes, cataloguing the strange asymmetry and the battered, pockmarked skin.

He flinched, turning away from her. "Nothin'."

But if his body language told her anything, it told her that the marks meant something to him.

"You won't tell me?"

With his head still down, he shrugged. "Nothin' to tell."

"Gardener," she said, taking one more step toward him. Gently, she tried to coax him to talk. "*Jardinier . . .*"

"Please," he muttered, as though asking for mercy. When he looked up, his expression was shrouded, troubled. "I don't want to talk about it."

But Jax wanted to talk about it. Suddenly she realized that she wanted to talk to him very much. She wanted to *know* this man who spoke French and planted moonlight gardens and used to "serve and protect." He had rescued her from danger and carried her like a doll in his arms on Saturday night, even though she was positive she annoyed him. He'd tenderly bandaged her wound and, despite his initial protests, he'd agreed to teach her how to defend herself. Not to mention he was one of a very few people on Blueberry Lane young enough to be her peer, to be her friend, to maybe—possibly—help thwart her loneliness.

Yes, she wanted to talk to him. Very much. Very badly.

Mustering her fragile courage, she said, "We could—we could be friends, you know. I only live two houses away . . . and you're going to be teaching me how to defend myself. I mean . . . we might as well be—"

He took a step back. "I don't think so, Duchess."

She grimaced, her feelings hurt. "Why not?"

He was scowling at her again, clenching his jaw tightly, his eyebrows knitted together in consternation. Finally he dropped her eyes, gesturing to the gym. "We can't be friends. We come from different worlds."

"Who cares?"

His head shot up, his eyes finding hers, searching them. "Don't *you*?"

"No."

"No?" he asked, his face registering genuine surprise. His lips twitched and his expression softened, giving her just enough encouragement to try again.

"I want to be friends," she answered, chancing a small smile and hoping he wouldn't crush it with whatever he said next.

He crossed his arms over his chest again, considering her for a long moment. "I don't have any friends who are women."

Her eyes widened and she laughed softly. "None?"

"Nope," he said. "Never tried it. Seemed dangerous."

It could be, she thought quickly before shoving the thought aside.

"You've dated, though?"

"Sure."

"And you weren't friends with any of your girlfriends?"

"I was," he said slowly, "but I was sleepin' with them, Duchess."

Her breath hitched and it felt like all the air was suddenly sucked out of the room. As appealing as that idea was, Jax wasn't the sort of girl who slept with men she barely knew.

"Well, you're *not* sleeping with me."

"Yet."

"Wh-what?" she stammered, her cheeks flushing pink.

"Uhhh . . ."

Putain de merde! he thought. *What the hell was that? Where did it come from?* And now that it was out there, he couldn't take it back. *God damn it!*

"*Yet?*" she squeaked.

"I just mean . . ."

He scrambled, trying to think of a way to back out of one stupid, tiny word that had just crossed a line he'd been so damn careful to observe up until now.

What *did* he mean? That he'd like to fuck her?

Yes. Of course. What man wouldn't? She was the perfect combination of pretty and hot—a bona fide knockout.

The problem, however, was that the time for an anonymous, gratuitous fuck had passed. He'd missed his chance on Saturday night when they were still virtual strangers and she'd offered him a kiss. Now? He'd gotten to know her a little: he knew she was vulnerable, hounded by the media, and—from what he could gather—lonely. The airspace for fucking her without any strings attached had already come and gone.

So the implication that they hadn't fucked . . . *yet*? It was awkward because it implied they would someday. And while that might sound like a fine idea to his dick, his head knew that it was just about impossible in real life. They were two broken creatures hiding from the world. They had no business making their lives more complicated by getting involved with each other.

He had no idea what to say, still wishing like hell that he could somehow rewind time and swallow his stupid "yet" before it had escaped his lips.

He'd been staring at the floor, but now he raised his eyes to apologize. Her wide green eyes still focused on his face with surprise, but as he stared back at her, he realized that her emeralds were twinkling. In fact, if he wasn't mistaken, she was trying not to laugh.

"*De ne pas coucher avec vos voisines*," she said, finally letting her smile break forth, accompanied by a soft chuckle.

Because there wasn't an exact translation in French for "Don't shit where you eat," she'd used the closest expression possible, which translated directly to "Don't sleep with your neighbors," which, in this particular situation, was so timely and so perfect, it made him throw back his head and laugh.

Not smirk. Not chuckle. But really *laugh* . . . which felt wonderful and weird and foreign, because as he stared at the ceiling listening to a rich bellow break free from his chest, he realized it had been ages since he'd heard the sound of his own laughter.

She joined him, giggling beside him for a moment before straightening, her blush deepening as she gestured awkwardly to the gym.

"Now we're even," she said, and he assumed she was referring to Saturday night when he turned her down for a kiss.

"Okay, Duchess. Even."

"Friends?" she asked, cocking her head to the side and holding out her hand.

Still smiling at her, admiring the way she'd let the whole episode roll off her back with humor, he nodded, pressing his hand to hers and pumping it once.

"Yeah, okay. Friends. You're cool, Jax," he said, trying out her nickname for the first time.

"And you barely know me," she said, tossing her ponytail over her shoulder with a sassy grin. "Just wait. I'm going to be the best friend you ever had, Gard."

Gard, huh? He was Gard now?

He raised his eyebrows, charmed by her and unable, or unwilling, to hide it for the moment. What was the point? They were going to be friends, right? He'd already surrendered.

"Really?"

"Really. After me, you're *only* going to want to be friends with women."

"I don't know about that."

"I promise."

"I doubt it."

"Why's that?" she asked, putting her hands on her hips and raising her pert little chin in challenge.

"Because we can't sit on a couch together watchin' a game, drinkin' beer, and belchin'. I'll still need a few guy friends for the truly disgustin' moments of male bondin'."

She gave him a look. "You forget. I grew up with two older brothers."

He scoffed. She was cool for letting the whole "yet" thing slide, and he was willing to couch their relationship in friendship if he was going to be training her over the next few weeks. But the duchess chugging a beer and burping her pleasure? Yeah, right. Not likely.

"Oh, you don't believe me, huh?"

"Nope."

"Not even a little bit?" she hummed, grinning at him like she knew something he didn't.

"Not even a little bit," he confirmed, straightening his smile and remembering why he was there. "Now, let's get back to the eyes, huh?"

For the following hour, they shelved the flirtation, and Jax was a surprisingly committed student, concentrating fully on his instruction. He taught her two techniques for startling and/or disabling her enemy: eye poking and eye gouging.

With eye poking, he explained, she should spread her second and third fingers and thrust them into her attacker's eyes, momentarily blinding him and hopefully giving her enough time to run away.

With eye gouging, he demonstrated how to grab your assailant's head and press your thumbs forcefully into his eye sockets with the intent of dislodging an eyeball.

Jax hesitated while performing both moves on the punching bag, which Gardener had expected, because poking or thrusting your fingers into the eyes of another human being was anathema to most people.

"I know it feels wrong to attack another creature's eyes. We're wired to reject it," he told her. "But these are two really useful moves and I need you to try, okay?"

Her jabs were pathetic at first, but by the end of the hour, she was trusting herself more. Using a punching bag as a "person," she was able to poke and gouge successfully several times.

One problem, however? For as good shape as she was in, Jax lacked the arm strength required to make either move truly effective.

He handed her two ten-pound dumbbells. "Time to build up some muscle mass in those arms."

As she took the weights from him, their fingers brushed together, and he'd be lying if he said he didn't feel it. He did. And it sent a tiny shiver of pleasure up his arm, making his hair stand on end, making his skin long for more contact. She must have felt it too because her eyes flared deep and green, and she gulped softly as she looked up at him.

"W-what do you want me to do with these?"

"Bicep curls," he said, pantomiming the movement and ignoring the annoying hint of gravel in his voice. "Twenty."

"Twenty," she said, lifting the weights from her hips to her shoulders.

"Shoulders back," he said by rote, instantly regretting the words as she followed his instructions and Jax's breasts, only covered by her blue sports bra, were thrust forward.

His eyes pinwheeled. His heartbeat quickened.

Blinking before looking away, he muttered, "Uh. Eighteen . . . seventeen . . . sixteen . . ."

"Gard . . ." she said between lifts, her voice breathy.

"Huh?" he asked.

"They're breasts. Half the population has them, including your mother and sisters."

They don't have yours, he thought, and even though the mention of his sisters and mother should have been enough to deflate things, it wasn't. His blood was already headed south. Fast. Very, very fast.

"Nine . . . eight . . ."

"Well, now that we're friends, you'll just have to stop noticing," she declared.

Like that was even a fucking possibility. He clenched his ass cheeks together, actively willing his dick not to swell anymore and begging the universe to shut down her voice box temporarily so she'd stop talking about her breasts.

Because one, they were fucking perfect.

And two, it had been way too long since he'd felt the warm weight of a woman's breast in his hand, and he missed it so fucking bad that his mouth watered.

"Four . . . three . . ."

She stopped at seventeen lifts, holding the dumbbells against her shoulders until he met her eyes. "Are you done?"

"With what?"

Her lips twitched, but she didn't let herself smile, tracking her eyes down to her breasts then back up again. "With whatever's going on here?"

Nope. He wasn't. Now that she was staring at him, her eyes flashing like jewels, surrounded by thick, dark lashes, he was in even more trouble. Exhaling the breath he was holding, he released his glutes and let nature do exactly what it wanted to do. His dick tented his sweats, and he could feel the throbbing knob pressed against his boxers, lifting the material of his pants. Well, so be it. There wasn't a fucking thing he could do about it now.

As Jax slowly lowered the weights, her eyes trailed down his chest, stopping at his hips. He watched as her lips parted, the way her teeth razed her bottom lip and her cheeks flushed crimson. A bead of sweat slipped from his hairline, sliding down the side of his face.

Lord, she was going to kill him.

"Oh," she murmured.

"Two," he growled.

She lifted the dumbbells, her eyes sliding back up, over his waist, so slowly he bet she could count the ridges in his chest. She paused for a moment at his throat, then met his glare.

"Apparently friends sometimes give friends hard-ons," he said sourly, pursing his lips.

Her eyes flared with surprise again and her shoulders started trembling. She let the weights fall to her sides as she started giggling.

He understood it was amusing to get a massive boner from talking about breasts, but she didn't know how long it had been since he'd been with a woman. He felt frustrated and embarrassed, out of control and annoyed. He needed a cold shower or a long walk, and getting naked and showering here at her gym didn't seem like a very good idea. She lifted and lowered the weights a final time and he took them from her, depositing them back on the rack.

"One," she said softly, and he wasn't sure if she was finishing off his curl count or counting the number of erections she'd given him. In the case of the latter, she was way off. Since meeting her on Saturday night, she'd given him at least half a dozen.

He headed for the gym door, grumbling, "I'll be back Wednesday, Jax" over his shoulder without looking back at his hot, sexy, funny, boner-inducing new "friend."

The door clicked shut behind him and Jax stared at it, her breathing shallow, her breasts rising and falling with each rapid breath.

She felt exhausted and exhilarated, unsatisfied and excited. Her lips still twitched, but now that he was gone, she didn't feel like laughing anymore.

Lesson one was over.

She reached for a bottle of water, took a sip, closed her eyes for a moment, then opened them again.

Lesson one was—*gulp*—over.

She looked at the door and sighed long and low.

Merde.

There was no point denying it: Jax Rousseau officially had a scorching crush on the Englishes' new gardener.

She moaned softly, remembering the roughness of his fingertips under her chin, the hunger in his eyes as he'd gazed at her, and later, the telltale bulge in his pants. He was tall and muscular with thick dark-blond hair and deep coffee-brown eyes that had seen better days.

And he was mysterious, this gardener with a past. How did someone born in New Orleans become a cop in Philly? Why had he left the South? Why had he stopped being a cop? What had happened to the skin around his eyes? She had so many questions and not enough answers. Who was this beautiful, enigmatic man who lovingly tended moonlight gardens but could also teach her how to disarm an assailant by gouging his eyes out? Gentle and lethal. Protective and taciturn.

One thing she knew for certain: they were both hiding from the world. She at her family's home, away from the prying eyes of a public she'd never intended to enamor. And he in a little studio tucked away on a grand estate, biding his time in a garden when he'd once had, according to Weston English, a decorated career.

Maybe that's why she was drawn to him so strongly—because they were both hiding, and she sensed that neither of them *wanted* to hide, but they had accepted their secluded existences because they *had* to. She didn't know for sure that she was right, but she felt inexplicably drawn to him, as though they shared a bleak commonality that made her feel a certain camaraderie toward him. She *liked* him. As the heat of his presence faded second by second with his absence, she felt the cold of her aloneness, her loneliness, surround her.

Buzz, buzz. Buzz, buzz.

Her cell phone sat on the table by the gym door buzzing.

"Hello?"

"Jax?"

"Hi, J.C.," she said, turning off the lights in the gym and heading through the door. "What's up?"

"I'm not good at this shit, so I'm going to cut to the chase."

"Ooooo-kay."

"Mad's worried about you. Chewed my fucking ear off in the car this morning. She thinks we need to get you into the city more often."

Jax walked through one of the sliding glass doors that led to the pool and sighed. "I'm fine."

"Yeah. That's what I said, but you know Mad."

She cradled the phone between her ear and shoulder, then reached for the waistband of her leggings, shimmying them down her legs until she stood on the pool deck in her sports bra and a pair of matching black-and-aqua boy shorts.

"I know Mad."

"She kept driving around until I promised I'd invite you to hang out. So . . . there's a game on tonight. Football."

"My fave," she said sarcastically.

She reached down for her leggings and threw them on a lounge chair, then stepped over the hot concrete to the stairs that led to the shallow end of the pool. Her father hadn't believed in heating outdoor swimming pools, so the water was icy cold on her feet.

"I'm heading to Mulligan's to watch it. You're welcome to meet me there if you want something to do."

Mulligan's. A popular hangout near UPenn that had satellite TV and showed all the European soccer games, or—as European purists like her brothers preferred to call it—football. She grew up watching them sit side by side on the couch in the den, beers in their hands, farting and belching as they exclaimed in French over every little—

Her eyes flew open and a smile spread slowly across her face as Gard's words resounded in her head: *Because we can't sit on a couch together watchin' a game, drinkin' beer, and belchin'.*

"What time does it start?" she asked eagerly, unable to mask her sudden rush of excitement.

"The game? Eight-thirty. Wow, Jax! I thought you hated football. I never thought you'd say yes!"

"I *do* hate football and I'm *not* saying yes," she said. "I have to go! *Je t'aime. Adieu!*"

"Jax? Jax! Wait a sec—"

But she was already out of the pool and hustling into the house. If they didn't have any beer in the house, she had just enough time to go into town and buy some.

Chapter 6

Dressed in jeans, a simple black V-neck T-shirt, and white tennis shoes, Jax walked across the lawns of Westerly at twilight, a six-pack of Big Easy IPA hanging from her fingers.

She'd jumped on the Internet to figure out if there were any breweries in Louisiana and had been delighted to learn that there was a very popular one, Abita, that distributed all over the country. And luckily, Haverford was the kind of town that had a posh liquor store with a walk-in cooler that sold beers from everywhere. She'd squealed with delight when she discovered not only several kinds of Abita beer available but a type actually called "Big Easy." It had felt like a sign.

Part of the reason she'd shut down Mad's suggestion about moving into Philadelphia was that there was a strong likelihood she'd be recognized there, and she couldn't bear it after the way her life had collapsed under the pressure of being constantly stalked in LA. Out here in Haverford, she felt relatively safe. No one had recognized her or bothered her during her short jaunt to the village, and she loved that measure of anonymity. She was finally breathing easier for the first time in months.

Crickets chirped noisily at Westerly, which smelled of cut grass and fresh mulch. A light summer breeze blew her loose hair off her shoulders and she breathed deeply, hoping this wasn't a massive mistake. Hmm. What exactly did she hope to get out of tonight?

She walked across the carpet of green as she mulled over the question. She felt safe at Le Chateau, but she also felt lonely . . . though she hadn't when Gard was there with her today. She wanted his friendship. Companionship. She wanted him to answer a few of the myriad questions she had about him. She liked looking at him. She felt a little thrill of victory every time he smiled or laughed instead of scowled or growled. Maybe he needed her just as badly as she needed him. And maybe it just felt nice to be needed.

Besides, friends drank beer and watched soccer together, right? Anyway, if he looked angry to see her, she could always play it off that she'd brought the beer as thanks for the lesson today. He couldn't object to that, could he? If it felt awkward, she could shove the six-pack at his six-pack and run home.

"Jax!"

Someone called her name from the back patio of Westerly, and Jax's thoughts scattered as she looked over to see Skye Sorenson Winslow, the wife of the eldest Winslow brother, Brooks, sitting in a wicker rocker with her two-month-old daughter, Sailor, in her arms.

"Hey, Skye," said Jax, waving at Brooks' wife.

Skye and Brooks seemed to be spending more time at Westerly since Sailor's birth, and Jax had run into her a few times. She got a good feeling from the no-frills, down-to-earth blonde. She just didn't know her very well. And suddenly it occurred to her that she didn't know anyone on Blueberry Lane very well . . . and wondered if she should consider remedying that. Especially if she planned to stay at Le Chateau for a little while.

Stepping over to the foot of the patio steps, she looked up and grinned. "Hope you don't mind that I'm cutting through."

"Not a bit! On your way to see the Englishes?"

"Um, yeah, I'm headed to Haverford Park," she said, hoping Skye would let her sidestep the question. She didn't feel like explaining that the Englishes' part-time gardener was teaching her self-defense and it was him Jax was visiting . . . the whole situation still felt strange to Jax, and part of her wanted to protect it by keeping it to herself. "How's Sailor?"

"Come see her," said Skye, her pretty face brightening at the mention of her tiny daughter.

Jax climbed the steps of the patio, setting the beer on the flagstone steps as she approached the mother and child. Nestled in a pink blanket, her eyes closed, her tiny fingers in a fist under her chin, was Sailor Winslow, fast asleep.

"Oh," sighed Jax as her heart tightened with a wave of unexpected longing. "She's beautiful."

"Mmmm," hummed Skye. "Right now she is. In a little while, when she's hungry, she'll be a holy terror."

Jax chuckled softly, lifting her eyes to Skye. "I know nothing about babies."

"Neither did I eleven months ago. That's why you're pregnant for nine months. It gives you time to learn everything."

Jax had never thought of that, but it made sense to her. She gestured to the grand house behind Skye. "How long are you three staying?"

"Well," said Skye, "I have some news, actually. Now that Sailor's here, we've decided to settle down and really make Westerly our home. My mother-in-law, Olivia, lives in London as you know, though she's welcome to visit whenever she likes. Brooks will still take sailing gigs now and then, but he's going to confine them to the Eastern Seaboard, and only for a week here and there."

"No more jaunts to Australia?" asked Jax.

Brooks Winslow was a world-renowned sailor and an Olympic medal winner who consulted for sailing teams all over the world. Because Brooks was several years older than she, Jax hadn't known him very well throughout her childhood, though she and Brooks' sister, Jessica, had been occasional playmates.

"Nope. No more. He's a family man now," said Skye. She leaned down and pressed her lips to Sailor's forehead. When she looked up, she smiled. "You know . . . I noticed you were staying at Le Chateau, and I've been meaning to ask you something. I'd like to, well, I don't know what exactly, but I'd like to host something, here at Westerly, you know? Sort of a summer party so people know we're living here now— that we're a permanent part of the neighborhood. I'd invite the Englishes, of course, and the Storys. Most of them live around here or in the city. I'd love for you, your brothers, and your sister to come too. We could have it in a few weeks when Kate and Étienne get home."

"Sounds like fun," said Jax, surprised that it actually *did* sound fun. She'd been so reticent to be out in public, her once-robust social life was now at a standstill. But Skye's party, with people she'd known all her life, behind the high walls of Westerly, with her siblings in attendance, would be safe from prying eyes. She could be herself. It could be a blast!

"What about the Amblers?" asked Skye, tilting her head to the side. "I don't hear very much about them."

"The . . . Amblers."

Jax thought about the family who owned the fifth and final house on Blueberry Lane, a sprawling farmhouse called Greens Farms across the street from the Englishes' estate, Haverford Park, and almost a full half-mile from the Storys' estate, Forrester. There was a reason Skye didn't know as much about the Amblers.

They'd long been the black sheep family of Blueberry Lane. While the Englishes, Winslows, Rousseaus, and Storys had reunited at every neighborhood cocktail party and local wedding, the Amblers were regarded as more Bohemian, free-spirited, or as Jax's father had observed more than once, "more flaky than a bowl of cereal."

Mariah and Theo Ambler were college professors, their minds steeped in and distracted by academia, leaving their four kids to run wild around the untended acres of their estate with seasonal au pairs trying unsuccessfully to keep order. Mrs. Ambler, née Coopersmith, came from old money, and a lot of it, but she'd rejected the Haverford lifestyle of country clubs and benefits, trading it for university life, wild and premature gray hair, and a near-constant look of absentmindedness. She hadn't encouraged her children to mix and mingle with the upper crust of Main Line society, and Jax strongly suspected she'd even discouraged it. As neighborhood children, they'd all known one another socially, and the Ambler children were sent to the same private Catholic school attended by the Rousseaus, Englishes, and Winslows, but with the exception of Bree, who was more Coopersmith than Ambler at heart, they didn't exactly move in the same circles anymore.

What made this news especially interesting to Jax, however, was the possibility of seeing Cortlandt Ambler once again. Jax and Cort had dated for one hot-and-heavy year of high school and broken up on the night of the junior prom. Since then, she'd seen him once or twice, but as far as she knew, he didn't spend much time, if any, at Greens Farms. Hmm. Cort. Did she want to see him again? Would he even show up to a party hosted by Brooks Winslow? Or would he look down his free-spirited, creative, Bohemian nose at his high-society neighbors?

"Sure," she said. "Invite the Amblers. Why not?"

"Brooks says they're kooky."

Jax giggled. "They are . . . a little."

"A splash of local color?" asked Skye with a minxy grin.

"The only splash of anything you'll find on Blueberry Lane," said Jax, thinking that the rest of them were pretty predictably upper class next to the "kooky" Amblers. "Are you thinking of doing a cocktail party?"

Skye grimaced. "That's not really me."

"You don't like cocktails?" kidded Jax.

"Sure I do. But a sleek, sophisticated party? I wouldn't even know where to begin. I didn't grow up here, Jax. My dad's a boat mechanic."

Jax shrugged because she truly didn't care what Skye's father did for work. It didn't alter her opinion of Skye Winslow to know her beginnings were modest. "So what are you thinking?"

"Well . . . what do you think about a movie night on the lawn?" asked Skye, her blue eyes sparkling hopefully. "I was thinking about *Wind*. It's a great sailing movie."

"That *is* sort of your thing," said Jax, grinning, remembering that Skye and Brooks had met at the marina where Brooks moored his sailboats.

Skye nodded with excitement. "I was thinking I'd have a caterer pass around little hot dogs and sliders . . . and maybe have a concession stand with a popcorn maker, candy, and cocktails."

"You could have green apple and candy apple martinis in green and red to represent port and starboard!"

"I love that idea!"

"And Daisy English could make you cookies in the shape of sailboats or sand dollars as party favors," said Jax, warming up to the idea.

"Oh! That's a great idea! I'll see her at Mommy and Me class tomorrow. I'll ask her!"

"Daisy's Delights is off the hook," said Jax.

Skye grinned in agreement. "Do you think I need to serve a sit-down dinner?"

Jax shook her head. "No way. Keep it casual. Passed hors d'oeuvres. I think you've got the perfect plan."

Skye looked like she was about to say something, then smiled and dropped Jax's eyes.

"Skye? What's up?"

Skye looked at Jax, a blush coloring her cheeks. "I know you're probably incredibly busy with movies and . . . I don't suppose you'd . . ."

"I'd what?"

Skye shrugged, looking sheepish. "Any chance you'd be willing to help me? I want it to be really fun and still look great, and I don't know if I trust myself."

"Sure." Jax chuckled, nodding her head. "I'd love to help."

Skye gasped. "Really? You would? You don't mind? You have time? I mean, you're a big Hollywood producer, and—"

"I'm sticking around here for a while," said Jax, "and I don't have a project right now. Plus, I think it sounds like a blast. I have a great projector in the screening room too. You're welcome to borrow it, or relocate to Le Chateau if it rains."

"Thanks! I'll take you up on that!"

Baby Sailor squirmed in her mother's arms, opening her rosebud lips to bellow with surprisingly sudden and white-hot anger. Her eyes fluttered open and her face reddened as she looked up at Skye.

"The terror awakens," said Skye, standing to maneuver a bawling Sailor to her shoulder. "I better take her inside to feed her. Can you come over Friday? Maybe for lunch? We'll get some ideas together."

Jax headed for the steps and picked up her six-pack. "Noon?"

"Perfect! I'll call Daisy English too!" said Skye, heading into the house. "Thanks, Jax. See you then!"

Jax watched her new friend head inside, Sailor's cries muffled as the door closed behind her, then she turned and hopped down the patio steps, feeling a lightness she hadn't enjoyed in a long, long time. Since moving home to Le Chateau, she'd thought of her childhood home as a temporary hiding place, but maybe it could be more. Maybe there was a new life to be found here if she chose to look for it. Besides, in the short term, she was good at planning parties, and seeing her childhood friends for a night of fun sounded promising.

The only thing she wondered, as she slipped through the hedges that bordered Westerly and Haverford Park, was whether or not she should bring a date.

Gardener had spent from four to eight o'clock weeding the formal rose garden and remulching it, and presently he was sitting in the rocker on his tiny porch with a cold bottle of water, taking his break before he'd spend another two hours planting more flowers in the moonlight garden before turning in. For some reason, he'd been thinking about jonquils this afternoon. Bright-white petals with a kiss of bright orange in the middle. He'd order them tomorrow from the local nursery and add them to the moonlight garden. Maybe around the base of the bench where he'd first met the duchess.

Scowling at himself for such fanciful thoughts, he took another gulp of water.

He was grateful for this job. His hours were loose—Felix understood that it was more comfortable for Gard to work in lower light and didn't seem to mind if Gard did most of his work in the late afternoon, evening, and night. He stopped by Gard's apartment every afternoon around one or two o'clock to touch base about what needed to be done, and so far the arrangement between the two men was working. Felix was still the head groundskeeper at Haverford Park, but Gard did a lot of the heavy lifting at night, which relieved a great deal of Felix's burden.

Meanwhile, Gard was supposed to be considering whether or not a life as Haverford Park's head groundskeeper could be his next step in life. And damn but he wished it felt like the next organic step for his life rather than a backup plan born from a shattered dream with skills he'd never really intended to use.

He leaned back in his chair and closed his eyes. It was a mellow evening with crickets chirping and the sound of a sprinkler *whoosh-whoosh-whooshing* in a rhythmic circle nearby. With the summer solstice only recently behind them, the sun was still brightening the sky even at 8:05, and a warm summer breeze blessed the skin of his face.

His face, which Jax had finally noticed, in all its gnarled ugliness, today. *His face*, the upper half of which was covered in the scars left behind by taking a sprinkle of birdshot to his forehead that had compromised his vision so irreparably that even after six surgeries, it was unlikely he would ever see clearly again.

He tipped the bottle to his lips and let the cold water sluice down his throat, unable to keep his dark memories at bay.

It had been an unseasonably chilly September day, almost two years ago, when he and his partner, Gil DeMarco, had approached Miguel Santiago's apartment in the rough Strawberry Mansion neighborhood of Philadelphia. As he pounded his fist on the Santiagos' door, he'd had no idea that it would be Gil's last day on earth and *his* last day as a whole man.

If he'd known, would he have done anything differently? Would he have ignored the screams of Carolina Santiago from inside the apartment and waited for backup? Probably not. Miguel was armed, she was in trouble, and if he and Gil had waited, her brother probably would have ended up shooting her. The only good that had come out of that horrible day was the fact that Carolina and her two young children had survived.

A sudden memory of Gil's face, partially blown off by the shotgun blast, flashed through Gard's mind, and he winced.

Don't go there, he told himself, his fingers clenched tightly around the plastic bottle. *That's an old chapter in a life that's over. Don't think about it. Think about something else.* Anything *else.*

With his eyes still closed, he took a deep breath, catching a whiff of something unexpected on the breeze . . . lemon, maybe. And a hint of rosemary. Wait a second . . .

He opened his eyes and there, standing in front of him, just over the railing, with a small grin on her beautiful face, was Jax Rousseau.

He stared at her, surprised by her sudden appearance and dumfounded by her beauty.

"Hi," she said softly.

He dropped his legs from the porch railing and leaned forward, resting his elbows on the railing and smiling back at her, gratitude for her sudden company welling inside of him like a burst of something very sweet and very bright in a dark, bitter life. Like a jonquil. Like a kiss of bright orange in the middle of quiet white.

She searched his eyes, her soft smile enchanting him. "What?"

"What?" he parroted, grinning back at her.

"You're looking at me funny."

"*Vous etes si belle que vous regarder est une souffrance,*" he whispered. *You're so beautiful, it hurts me to look at you.*

"Oh," she murmured, her lips parting as she gazed back at him. Finally she shrugged—the barest motion of one shoulder grazing the delicate lobe of her ear. "*Merci.*"

Frissons of excitement and awareness leapt between them, making him sit up straighter, pay attention, drink in the sight of her. She wore her hair down for the first time he could remember—long, silken tresses parted in the middle of her head, falling past her shoulders in dark waves. Her lips were shiny, and a simple black T-shirt covered her breasts. She was as natural as he'd ever seen her, but so lovely, she didn't seem real.

"Nice night for sitting outside," she said.

He nodded, staring at her glossy lips and picking up the scent of the gloss she wore. Coconut? No. Pineapple. His mouth watered. "Yep."

They stared at each other in silence for several seconds before Jax looked down, shifting her weight back and forth. It was a tell, he realized. She was trying to gather her courage to do or say something, and she wasn't sure how he'd respond. It made him feel a little bad, that, because it meant he'd probably hurt her with a gruff response or two over the last few days. It made him angry at himself, because when he hurt her, her eyes lost a little of their cautious shine, and the more time he spent with her, the more he hated seeing that happen.

"What's up, Jax?" he asked softly.

"I, uh . . ." She cleared her throat. "Remember what you said today? About how you'd need to find a friend to watch games with?"

"Uh-huh. Somehow I don't see you fillin' that need, Duchess."

She held up the six-pack of Abita, resting it on the railing about an inch from his nose. "Don't be so sure."

His eyes focused on the cardboard box, and he felt a beaming smile pulling at his lips, crinkling his eyes and lightening his heavy heart. "Abita."

"It's from Louisiana."

"You bought Abita."

She cringed. "Good or bad?"

Gard massaged his bristly chin with his thumb and forefinger, his mouth watering. "Good, Jax. Very, very good."

"You like it?" she asked, her voice high with an excited squeal.

"*Beaucoup*." He took the beer and stood, looking down at her as he gestured to the door with his chin. "You comin' in?"

She nodded. "If I'm invited."

"You're invited, Duchess."

He opened the door and stepped into the small living room area, setting the six-pack on the coffee table and heading to the kitchen for two glasses. He didn't know why she was here again, and honestly, he didn't care. Five minutes before she'd arrived, he'd been alone with his terrible memories. Now he was about to share a bottle of his favorite beer with a gorgeous woman who wanted nothing more complicated than to be his friend. Looked at in the right light—the light that didn't include the way his heart started racing whenever he locked eyes on her—he was one lucky bastard.

"You want a glass?"

"No, thanks," she said. "I'll drink it from the bottle."

He put the glasses back in the cabinet and turned to face her.

She'd surprised him. Again.

"Really?"

"Yeah. If that's okay with you."

"Whatever you want."

He opened a drawer, feeling around for the bottle opener he kept there, then joined her. He sat across from her, in one of two easy chairs, while she sat on her usual sofa-edge perch. The bottles hissed as he popped the caps off, and he lifted the cold glass to his lips, unable to keep from groaning with pleasure as the bubbles slipped down his throat.

Home. Glory Lord, it tastes like ever-lovin' home. All the good bits without the bad.

When he opened his eyes, she was watching him with interest, her eyes wide and soft.

"What?" he asked.

"*Vous etes si belle que vous regarder est une souffrance,*" she answered, giving him a small, disarming grin before tilting her own bottle back.

His eyes registered shock, and she wondered if it was the same jolt of awareness she'd felt when he'd said the same words to her in his dark, rough, Cajun-accented French. If so, he deserved it. Her stomach hadn't stopped fluttering since.

She didn't know what was going on between them. Hell, they'd only met each other a few days ago, but suddenly she felt like she was in the middle of something bigger than a flirtation or acquaintance, and it surprised her to discover there was nowhere else she'd rather be.

"Tell me about makin' a movie," said Gard, rolling the bottle rim along his full lower lip.

She took a deep breath and sighed. The last thing she wanted to talk about was movies, because talk of movies invariably led to talk of her *next* movie, and Jax wasn't sure what came next in her life, movies or otherwise. All she knew was that the entire conversation felt daunting and left her anxious.

"There's a soccer game on," she said. "We could just—"

"You like soccer?" he asked her, his eyes narrowing as he cocked his head to the side.

"Sure," she said, but she knew immediately her tone wasn't convincing, because he chuckled.

"About as much as a root canal, eh, Duchess?"

"You wanted a friend who'd drink beer with you and—"

"I don't need you to be that friend, Jax. Just be yourself."

Just be yourself.

Just be yourself.

Tears filled her eyes without permission and a huge lump formed in her throat.

Just be yourself.

Such easy advice . . . if you knew who that was.

"Jax?"

"I lost her," she said softly.

"Who?" he asked, his forehead creasing in confusion.

"Whoever I was before . . . before . . ."

"Before makin' the movie," he said slowly, lowering his bottle.

She nodded.

"Well . . . what do you recall of her? What did you like about her?"

"She was carefree. She was fun-loving. She was strong."

"Those sound like good things," he said.

"They were." Jax paused, feeling a bleakness envelope her as she told him about the girl she used to be. "She went to parties and posted silly pictures on Facebook and Instagram. She lived in LA."

"Did she like that?" He asked, taking a long draw on his beer. "Goin' to parties and livin' in a big city?"

Jax took a deep breath.

"I was *supposed* to like it, but . . ."

"But?"

"No."

The word came unbidden but easily.

"Why not?"

"I . . . I missed the country. The dark nights. The sounds of crickets in the evening and black-capped chickadees in the morning. The smell of cut grass. The space to breathe. I mean, the partying? It *looked* fun, but it wasn't. It was either assholes like Tripp groping me or people I barely knew acting like we were best friends. It was all fake. I had no . . . anchor. Not in that world." She took a deep breath, remembering the crowds of photographers who'd started following her after the Oscars. "When the paparazzi started hounding me, there was no one to protect me, no one who made me feel safe. My family was here, so far away. I didn't want a bodyguard, but I hired one, and he sold pictures of me sleeping . . . to the *Star News*."

"*Salaude*," he muttered under his breath, his expression murderous. *Bastard.*

"Exactly." She shrugged. "And you know the worst? I didn't even know until I stopped by the grocery store to pick up a few things and saw myself on the cover. They said I was passed out drunk in the caption, but I wasn't. I was just . . . sleeping."

"I'm sorry." He flexed his jaw, his narrowed eyes searching her face without judgment. "Keep goin'. Tell me more about that girl."

Jax sat back a little, taking a sip of beer, then backhanding her lips in thought. "She wasn't sure where she was going. I mean, she wasn't sure what she wanted to do with her life. She'd graduated college with honors six years ago, but she hadn't found her thing yet, and then—"

"Her *thing*?"

"You know . . . the thing she wanted to do with her life. She'd tried raising horses. She'd tried becoming a lawyer. She'd tried the family business . . ."

"And she tried makin' a movie."

Jax nodded. "She did."

"And . . . did she like it? *Any* of it?"

"She loved horses, but not breeding them. She loved her brothers, but not working with them. She liked that *studying* the law gave her purpose and direction, even though she didn't love the law itself. She *loved* making *The Philly Story*," she said in a passionate whisper, looking up at him, meeting the intense gaze in his dark eyes. "She loved it more than anything."

"But you didn't love livin' in . . ."

"Beverly Hills," she said.

"Well, there've got to be lots of ritzy suburbs outside of LA, right? So buy a house in one of those neighborhoods and get out of the city."

It wasn't a bad idea, but since she'd returned home to Haverford, she couldn't imagine leaving it again. And that was when she made her decision—right then and there with a cold bottle of Abita in her hand and this beautiful man she barely knew helping her sort out her life: whatever plans lay ahead for Jax, they didn't include returning to LA. She was staying in Haverford near her family. And a burden lifted from her heart as she felt the rightness of her decision.

Gard continued. "You said you didn't like constant partyin'. The people who surrounded you in that life."

She shook her head. "I didn't."

"You're well rid of it then. Be more choosy about the parties you attend. And make some real friends. Find people who care about you, who will . . . anchor you, protect you, make you feel safe."

She nodded, loving these words, *her* words, falling from his lips. "Yes."

He continued. "You didn't like the business of breedin' horses, but you liked the animals themselves. You didn't like the family business, but you love your family."

"Right." She leaned forward, rapt. "So . . . ?"

"So move to the suburbs, stop partyin', find some solid friendships, buy a few horses, and make time for your family."

"Is it that easy?" she asked.

He shrugged. "I don't know why not. World's your oyster, Duchess."

Wide-eyed and stunned, she stared at him, breath escaping her throat to utter a single word. "Yes!" A happy giggle bubbled up through her throat "Okay! I will." She beamed at him. "Then what?"

He furrowed his brow for a moment. "Well, since you loved makin' a movie . . . make another."

Her shoulders deflated. Her hopeful smile inverted into a frown. "No."

"Why not?"

"Because movies are made in LA, and I don't want that—"

"That life? You don't have to have *that life*," he said. He lifted his beer and took a long sip, the muscles in his throat working as Jax stared at him, mesmerized. Finally he lowered the bottle and grinned at her. "Duchess, buildin' a life is about takin' the pieces that matter and figurin' out how to fit them together. You already know what you want. So fit them together."

She cocked her head to the side. "Is that what you've done? By quitting your job and coming here?"

"I didn't quit." His eyes, which had been warm and helpful, shuttered closed. When he opened them again, they were significantly cooler. "Anyway, we're not talkin' about me."

"Why not?" asked Jax, whose questions for and about Gardener Pierre Thibodeaux felt endless. "Let's talk about you."

Chapter 7

Gard stared back at her, uncertain of how to respond, his annoyance quick and hot.

She had stumbled into his life on Saturday night, but since then she'd been like a bad penny, turning up again and again, contriving ways to see him and talk to him and insert herself into his life. Her body distracted him. Her unhappiness bothered him. Her presence shined a light on the shortcomings in his own life, and he didn't feel like looking at them. And in such moments as these, his first instinct was to tell her to get lost.

But then he remembered how he'd felt right before she'd showed up this evening and realized he didn't want her to go. He didn't know what was going on between them—he was definitely attracted to her and he was fairly certain she was attracted to him. He lived ten minutes away from her and had promised to teach her self-defense in very close and private quarters. She said she wanted to be friends, and while he really didn't know how that would look, he also knew that whether it was Jax Rousseau or someone else, he'd become a hermit if he didn't open up a little to *someone*. He missed having friends to talk to, and if he didn't see them anymore, he may as well talk to the pushy neighbor who wouldn't leave him alone.

So he didn't tell her to get lost.

But he did stall. He stood up and headed to the kitchen for another beer.

"Want another, Duchess?"

"Sure," she said. When he turned around, she chugged the bottle in her hand, as though fulfilling a dare he hadn't actually issued.

He handed her the cold, open bottle and sat back down across from her. "What do you want to know?"

She looked surprised for a moment, like she'd been expecting him to get all pissed off and throw her out, and a sweet little smile played at the delectable corners of her mouth. *Lord, it would be easier to just make out and skip talking about deep things like life and the future.*

"Really?"

He shrugged, taking a long sip and trying to look like it didn't matter to him.

"Okay . . . ," she said, "you're from New Orleans. How'd you end up in Philly?"

"I got a full scholarship to St. Joseph's."

Jax whistled low. "Wow. That's great. For what?"

"Sports." He chuckled softly. "Soccer, actually."

"Soccer," she said. She cocked her head to the side. "So why aren't you watching the game?"

"'Cause I'm talkin' to you, Duchess."

A splash of pink appeared on her cheeks as he drawled this line slow and low, and he couldn't help but admire his handiwork. He liked that he affected her. He liked it too goddamned much.

"So you come to Philly, you attend St. Joe's, you study . . . ?"

"Double major. English and criminal justice."

"Of course. And play soccer."

He nodded. "When I graduated, I decided to stay, so I—"

"Why?" she asked. "Why'd you stay? Why didn't you go home to Nawlins?"

He had to hand it to her: her accent wasn't half bad.

"Because of a girl," he said, seeing no good reason to lie. She'd trusted him with her truth; the least he could do was trust her with his.

He leaned forward to grab his beer, and if he hadn't looked up when he did, he would almost have missed it: the slight narrowing of her eyes and pursing of her lips. Jealousy. He'd stake his life on it. He grinned at her. "Don't worry. Didn't work out, Duchess."

"I'm *not* worried," she said, lifting her chin and wrinkling her nose.

The hell you're not, he thought, feeling unaccountably pleased that he'd made her jealous.

"What happened?"

"Doesn't matter."

"What was her name?"

"Doesn't—"

"—matter. Right." She frowned at him but finally let it go. "So it didn't work out with *whatshername,* but you . . . ?"

"I was already livin' here, already workin' here. Movin' up in the department. Had friends. So I stayed."

"Didn't you miss your family?"

"They have their own lives."

She frowned. "Do you go home to visit?"

Gard took a deep breath and sighed. His father, Lord bless him, had passed away three years ago, leaving an aching place in Gard's heart. He'd loved and admired his father, and they'd been good friends. Sure, he loved his mother and sisters, but he didn't have the camaraderie with any of them that he'd had with his dad.

His mother was involved in her ladies' card groups and charities. His sisters were both married with children. He hadn't kept up with his high school friends, and besides, he'd been in a weird social place growing up: his father made enough money that they were considered wealthy, but Cadogan Thibodeaux made his money dirtying his hands with soil and mulch while most of the fathers of his peers in private Catholic school made their money in finance or law. Gard's childhood home had been big and showy, putting off the working-class, scholarship kids, but he was new money, and his parents reeked of it, which had put off the upper-class kids, like Jax's kind. He'd grown up in no man's land. Moving to Philadelphia, where he could just be himself, had been a relief. There were things about New Orleans he'd always love, but going home permanently had never been part of his plan. And anyway, he felt his dad's loss a hell of a lot more there than here.

Do you go home to visit?

"At Christmas."

"You have friends at home?"

"Not really."

"Here?"

He shrugged.

"Sort of a loner, huh?"

He considered this for a second. In high school, yes, he'd been somewhat of a loner for the reasons he'd already recalled, but that had changed little by little in college, and for good when he'd become a cop. He'd had lots of friends in the department with whom he worked and played in a weekend soccer league sponsored by the city. But since the accident, he hadn't sought out those friends—for one thing, he couldn't see worth a damn, so he wasn't any use on the soccer field anymore. But more importantly, being around those guys made him think of Gil, which made him feel guilty, made him feel bad and angry, made him feel so damned resentful of everything he'd lost.

"Wasn't always," he finally answered.

Jax took a sip of her beer, then set it down on the table in front of her with a *plunk*. "*Merde!* Getting answers out of you is like pulling teeth."

"And here I thought I was bein' downright chatty."

"No," she said, crossing her arms over her chest. "You're being infuriating."

"How's that?" he asked, confused, wondering why the hell she'd gotten so mad so fast.

"Every little tiny answer leads to ten more questions."

"Like what?"

"Like . . . why aren't you closer to your family? Do you still play soccer? Why aren't you a cop anymore? Do you or do you not have friends? And what happened with the girl?"

"None of your business."

"You're not good at this!" she said in a huff, standing up.

"At *what*?" he asked, following her lead and standing up across from her, his hands on his hips.

"Being friends! If we're going to be friends . . . I mean, friends talk and—and share stuff."

"Believe it or not, Duchess, I just shared more with you than I have with anyone since . . ."

"Since . . . ?"

Since my best friend was shot and I lost the lion's share of my eyesight. Since my whole life changed in the blink of an eye.

"You look tired," he said calmly, using the tone of voice his father had always employed with great success when one of Gard's sisters was in a snit. "Let's call it a night."

"Ooooo!" she snarled, her emeralds wide and angry. "Maddening! Since *what*? Since *when*?"

He didn't know what bee flew into her panties, but she was acting like a brat. He pointed a finger at her, feeling his temper rise. "You're pushy and rude, you know that?"

"I'd say you *need* a push," she shot back.

"And you're just the one to give it to me, huh?"

"Maybe," she said, flashing her eyes at him.

He steeled his expression, his voice low and serious. "I'm not your project while you're between gigs, Duchess."

"I—I never said you were."

But her voice was weak and her eyes betrayed her.

He was a little.

He'd known it too, but he hadn't minded it as much when it was unspoken. Now? It pissed him off, in part because he saw her as his project too, and he wasn't sure how he felt about this unspoken agreement between two injured birds still wishing they could fly. It felt dangerous suddenly, like talking about all this was something that could hurt him or hurt her, like maybe a quick retreat would be a good idea right about now.

"Come on . . . I'll walk you home," he said, hooking his thumb at the door but opting for a gentler tone.

Without arguing, she took a step toward the door and he followed her. But before she walked through, she turned and leaned against it, looking up at him, her arms still crossed over her chest, her breasts heaving over her forearms with the force of her agitated breathing.

"I don't want to leave," she said, her eyes troubled, her brows furrowed.

He stared at her, raising his eyebrows in frustration. "What *do* you want?"

"Tell me what happened with the girl," she said quietly, her eyes searching his.

"Why does it matter?"

"It just does."

He shook his head back and forth, annoyed with her and even more annoyed with himself, because when she asked all quiet and serious like that, he found he couldn't refuse her. "I found her with my partner. My first partner, Brad."

"*Found* her?"

"In my apartment. *Our* apartment. In *our* bed."

Her mouth opened to a perfect *O* shape, and to his great surprise, he found he was far more distracted by Jax's lips than upset by old memories of Tiffany's betrayal.

He nodded. "Yeah. There you go. Now you know. I hope you're happy."

"Oh . . . no. I'm not. I'm—I'm sorry."

He winced. Pity. His least favorite emotion. And he couldn't—wouldn't—stand for it from her. For some reason, pity from the duchess was absolutely unacceptable.

"Time to go," he muttered.

She flinched. Her eyes were soft in the dim light, bright green and regretful. Vulnerable. Beautiful. God damn it, he didn't want her fucking pity. He wanted her—

"Gardener," she whispered, reaching out to flatten her hand on his chest, directly over his heart, her unexpected touch effectively ending his train of thought. "Listen. I'm sorry for asking. For pushing. For being rude. For—for being a bad friend. I said you weren't good at this and then I . . . I go ahead and . . ."

He'd been holding his breath, but now he released it in a low hiss. Fuck. She wasn't sorry *for him*. She was sorry for her behavior. Half of him wished she'd said, "I'm sorry your girlfriend cheated on you," because her pity would have made it easy to push her out the door. The fact that she was apologizing for her *own* actions instead of pitying his past, however, made him feel relieved, made him step forward instead of away, his eyes dropping to her lips.

"You were right," he whispered, inclining his head to hers. "I'm not good at this."

His lips touched down gently on hers, trapping her top lip and pursing its softness between his. A breathy "ahhh" sound released from the back of her throat made him move his lips again, this time capturing the bottom one for a long moment before releasing it. Her hand moved to his chest, flattening beside the other, her nails curling just slightly into his shirt as he deepened the kiss.

The smell of lemons and rosemary invaded his senses and he closed his eyes, sealing his lips over hers as he pulled her into his arms. She fit easily against him, slipping her hands up his chest and around his neck. Her breasts, crushed against his pecs, made his dick swell against her hips. Tentatively he touched his tongue to hers, and when she moaned into his mouth, he clutched her tighter, sliding his tongue along the length of hers, exploring her mouth, which tasted sweetly of IPA and the pineapple of her lip-gloss. He skimmed one hand up her back, over her T-shirt, sliding his fingers into her soft mane of hair and tilting her head back to give his mouth a better, more dominant angle over hers. And she leaned back against the arm still around her waist, submitting to him, letting him ravage her mouth the way he wished he could ravage her sweet body.

"*Duchesse, Duchesse, Duchesse*," he murmured, trailing his lips down the hot, throbbing skin of her throat, feeling her beaded nipples pushing against the muscles of his chest. Her pulse beat wildly and her breasts thrust up against him with every shallow breath. She was panting as hard as he was, as turned on, as undone.

Letting his fingers go slack in her hair, he lowered his hand, holding her tightly against his body as her forehead dropped to the crook of his neck and rested there. It felt good—so good to hold her, to feel the warmth of her body against his and the whisper of her sweet, soft breath dusting his skin. It had been so long . . . so long . . .

"Gardener?"

Her voice was breathless and soft, a reminder that she was vulnerable and lonely, and a sudden wave of guilt washed over him as his body tensed. What the *hell* was he doing? Was this okay with her? Was this what *she* wanted? Fuck, they barely knew each other and he was kissing her like he had a right, like she'd given him permission . . . and she hadn't.

He cleared his throat. "Jax . . . I didn't mean to—"

She jerked her head back to look up at him, her eyes severe. "*Don't* apologize. Don't be sorry."

Her reaction surprised him, but in an instant he realized that apologizing to her would read the same way to her as her pity would read to him.

"I'm not sorry," he said quietly.

He hoped that he was convincing. He hoped she didn't hear the lie in his voice. Because he *was* sorry. He was sorry he knew what it was like to hold her, to kiss her. He was very sorry because the real thing was so much better than his fantasies, and his fantasies had been enough to keep him awake two nights in a row. Yes, he was sorry.

"Good," she said, her face still worried as he released his grip on her. "Because we can still be friends. It's still—I mean . . . it was just a kiss, right? A blip. No big deal."

Just a kiss? A blip? No big deal? He concealed a flinch by rubbing the back of his hand over his lips. It hurt a little that she said that, because, surprisingly, it had felt like a bigger deal to him. He hadn't kissed someone in a long time, and kissing her had felt so . . . right.

She was still staring up at him, waiting for him to answer. He folded his arms across his chest and forced an expression of boredom, like he kissed gorgeous neighbors every day.

"Sure. Sometimes friends kiss each other," he said, unable to keep a bite out of his tone.

Still watching him, she opened the door and took a step back onto his porch. "There's still some light. You don't need to walk me home."

"Whatever you want," he said, hating his weakness when his glance slipped to her still-slick lips. He looked away quickly.

"So, um, good night?" she whispered, her voice ending on a little squeak.

He looked up at her, catching the uncertainty in her eyes, the way she searched his face like she was looking for something. And damned if he knew what it was. She didn't want an apology, and hell, he'd wanted to kiss her from the very first moment he'd laid eyes on her, dressed like a duchess in the moonlight. So fine, he'd gotten his kiss and he wouldn't apologize for it. But clearly, kissing him hadn't meant anything to her. Which was fine. She was probably one of those rich chicks who kissed guys for sport. It didn't matter that it was the sweetest kiss he'd ever had. She wasn't into it being anything more than a blip. Good. Fine. It would be that much easier for him to be sure it didn't happen again.

"'Night, Duchess."

She paused, looking like she wanted to say something else, but when she finally did, it was just to confirm her next self-defense lesson. "See you Wednesday? At three?"

He nodded curtly in response.

Then she turned, stepped down the porch steps, and disappeared into the dying light.

Jax dreamt of Gardener.

His hands on her skin.

His tongue in her mouth.

The hardness of his erection pressed against her jeans.

She woke up in the half-light of early dawn, her fingers already under her panties, sliding into her soaked folds, her breathing shallow and quick. She could still feel the heat of his lips on hers, the hot skin of his neck under her fingertips, the strength of his arms around her. It didn't take long for her to orgasm, her head sinking into the pillow and hips bucking off the bed as she came. She licked her dry lips as her breathing slowed to normal, listening to the rain outside and wondering when it had started.

Her walk back to Le Chateau last night had been cool but dry, her mind whirling as she'd walked alone in the twilight reliving every second of their kiss. She'd wanted him to kiss her since Saturday, and now he had, but it hadn't quenched her thirst for him. All she wanted was more.

She was lying through her teeth when she said that it was no big deal. But she couldn't bear his apology, and even though he'd said he wasn't sorry, his eyes had said otherwise. He *was* sorry. She could tell. All she'd wanted to do was take the pressure out of the situation and let him know she was cool enough to kiss a man and not expect anything else. Better to beat him to the punch and let him know it didn't mean anything rather than bear the humiliation of his regret.

But it *had* meant something. A lot of something. In fact, it was by far the best kiss she'd ever had.

Taking a deep breath, she closed her eyes and sighed, remembering her surprise when he'd suddenly bent his head and captured her lip between his, gently tugging and pulling before letting it go and loving the other. And when his tongue had slipped between her lips? *Ah, merde.* She'd wanted it to go on forever. If he hadn't stopped, she might have stayed all night long, a thought that made her shiver with longing.

After their workout, when his body had—*ah-hem*—showcased his attraction to her, she thought that maybe they were both interested in something more . . . but no. It had just been biology, not a specific interest in her. He was just a big flirt, and he probably had that reaction whenever he worked out with a woman. If she'd been the lady her mother had raised, she wouldn't have noticed it. Frowning, she rolled to her side and beat her pillow into submission with her fist before laying her head back down.

She'd practically thrown herself at him since the moment she'd stumbled into his stupid garden, but no more. He was her neighbor and her trainer and that was all.

Well, not all, she thought, her lips twitching with irritation. He'd actually been a pretty decent friend tonight when she was telling him about her life.

. . . move to the suburbs, stop partyin', find some solid friendships, buy a few horses, and make time for your family . . . since you loved makin' a movie . . . make another.

With an annoyed huff, she sat up in bed and looked over at her desk, which was surrounded by UPS and FedEx boxes that had been forwarded to Le Chateau from her apartment building in LA.

Purposely ignoring them, she slipped out from under her duvet and walked to the French doors that led to a balcony. She opened the doors to the cool, damp early-morning air, closing her eyes and breathing deeply.

. . . you loved makin' a movie . . . make another . . .

"You don't have all the answers," she said aloud, her eyes popping open. "You don't even know me!"

. . . make another . . .

She stepped back onto the plush cream-colored carpet she'd chosen in high school and crossed her arms over her chest, looking at the pile of boxes.

. . . buildin' a life is about takin' the pieces that matter and figurin' out how to fit them together.

She padded across the room and knelt down on the floor next to the boxes, picking up the first one, ripping the tear strip, and flipping the box over so that a bound script fell into her lap. She pushed the cover letter aside to see the title: *The Sultan's Surrender.*

"Ugh," she groaned, reaching for another box.

Give It to Me One More Time.

"C'mon!" she muttered.

Another.

Lady and the Trump.

She rolled her eyes and grabbed another, ripping the strip open.

Shipwrecked.

Another.

Forever My Girl.

"*C'est des conneries!*" she cursed, looking through the pile for something that looked different, that looked real, that looked interesting and provocative, not just sensational drivel.

And then she saw it: a plain, white, unassuming envelope with local postage and a Philadelphia postmark. Pushing two other boxes aside, she pulled the white package from the pile and opened the envelope, flipping over the script and reading the title: *Philadelphia Vice.*

Hm.

Scooting away from the pile of hopefuls and rejects, Jax leaned her back against the leg of her desk and opened the script.

Three hours later, she was breathless with excitement, jerking her head up with surprise when Mrs. Jefferson, her mother's housekeeper, entered her room with a pot of coffee, fried eggs, and toast on a breakfast tray.

"Morning, Ms. Rousseau," she said, heading for the balcony, where Jax preferred to take her breakfast. "Looks like someone's been up for a while."

"Good morning, Mrs. Jefferson!" said Jax, realizing for the first time that her room was bright with morning sun. "What time is it?"

"Breakfast time. Eight-thirty," she said, setting up Jax's breakfast on the small two-person bistro table outside. She'd brought a towel to dry off the tabletop and one chair. "Rain stopped an hour ago. It's a beautiful morning!"

Still gripping the script, Jax stood up and stretched, leaning her neck from side to side to get the kinks out. "I've been reading."

Mrs. Jefferson nodded, surveying the mess of tear strips, open boxes, and discarded scripts strewn on the floor around Jax's desk. "I see."

She shrugged sheepishly, holding *Philadelphia Vice* against her chest. "Might have found a winner."

"A new movie?" asked the older woman with a surprised smile.

Jax shook her head. "No. TV."

"Well, now. I didn't know you produced TV shows," said Mrs. Jefferson, heading back toward Jax's bedroom door.

"I've never tried," said Jax. "But . . ."

"There's a first for everything," said Mrs. Jefferson, giving Jax a kind smile before she slipped from her bedroom.

"Yes," said Jax, placing the script on the table across from her like a dining companion and picking up her coffee cup with a bemused grin. "Yes, there is."

Chapter 8

Gardener's walk to Le Chateau was much faster on Wednesday afternoon, partly because he knew the way through the hedgerow and partly because he was irritatingly eager to get there. He hadn't seen Jax since their kiss on Monday night and—fuck *him*—it had felt like a long time. He'd pathetically hoped she'd show up on Tuesday night with another six-pack of Abita and that they'd both admit that the kiss they'd shared was a lot more than a blip, but no such luck. The rain showers from Tuesday morning had returned by dusk, and he'd spent the evening alone and ornery, missing her company and hating himself for it.

Without much else in the way of distraction, he'd had plenty of time to think about her over the last couple of days—Jacqueline Rousseau. Jax. The duchess. She was something, all right, with her black hair and green eyes, her tight little body and endless questions. He'd never met anyone quite like her.

He hadn't dated much in high school, finding himself stuck in no man's land between two distinct classes of Southern society that didn't mix it up much. And for the first two years of college, he'd been quietly fascinated with Northern girls. Not that he didn't know half a dozen Southern girls who could shotgun beers on the backs of their boyfriends' tractors while mudding on a sunny afternoon, but Northern girls were different in their version of brashness. There was something he liked about their interrogation-style conversation, even though he was still getting used to it ten years later. The way Northern girls volunteered so much information about themselves took away a certain amount of feminine mystique and leveled the playing field between men and women in a way he liked, in a way that felt equitable to him. He also liked it that Northern girls seemed more comfortable in their own skin—unlike his mother and sisters, for example, who hit the beauty salon and nail place every Saturday morning like clockwork. In all the time he and Tiff were together, he only remembered her getting her nails done once in a while for special occasions.

Tiffany.

He'd been thinking about her a bit over the past two days too.

Paired up as lab partners junior year at St. Joe's with a scorching personal chemistry that was immediately apparent, they'd wasted no time "getting to know each other," making out the first day they met and essentially spending every waking moment together thereafter. It had been good too—for a while. He'd loved having someone to spend time with, someone to fall asleep next to him and wake up beside him in the morning. The summer break between junior and senior years was interminable, but their relationship was as strong as ever when they returned to SJU in the fall, picking up exactly where they'd left off in June. It was like he was built to be half of a couple, and he reveled in having her by his side.

After graduating, they'd both found jobs in Philly—Tiff as a paralegal at a law office, while Gard had applied to the Philadelphia Police Department. After passing several tests and examinations, he'd attended the training program and become a police officer 1.

During Gard's year of probation, he'd been paired up with a seasoned cop, Brad Bender, who'd been on the force for eight years and had a wife and two kids. Little did Gard know that when Brad asked Gard to "man the grill" at weekend BBQs that included lots of guys from the force, Brad and Tiffany were meeting up inside the house for a quick fuck. Essentially, while Gard manned the grill, Brad manned Tiffany.

They eventually got so comfortable, *and sloppy*, they moved their extracurricular activities to Tiffany and Gard's apartment and met there during their lunch breaks because it was closer to the precinct. One day, when Gard took an elbow to the face and was sent home early with a broken nose, he'd gotten a broken heart in the bargain too. He found Brad—his mentor, his partner, his friend, his brother—balls deep in Tiffany.

Crossing in front of Westerly, Gard ran a hand through his hair. That was six years ago, and in the time since, he'd fucked some but loved none. His one big foray into love had sucked, and whether it was a conscious decision or not, he'd steered clear of it since.

Which is why he'd decided that it was also better to steer clear of Jax Rousseau. Because that rush of intense feeling he'd felt for Tiffany in junior year chemistry had come back in spades since he met Jax. She was beautiful and smart, and Lord but it felt good to be needed. He'd known in his gut—the first time he laid eyes on her—that the duchess could be no passing fancy used to scratch an itch or spice up the dog days of summer. Gard knew his heart. And with Jax Rousseau, it would eventually come down to all or nothing. And he'd just as soon avoid the all to sidestep the inevitable nothing.

Cruising through the hedgerow with ease, he turned left and followed the flagstone path to the front of Le Chateau, bypassing the small set of steps that led to the study and climbing up the wide marble steps just beyond that led to a set of three French doors. Pressing the doorbell, he straightened his spine and crossed his arms over his chest.

To his surprise, the door wasn't opened by Jax. He was greeted by a middle-aged woman wearing black pants and a crisp white shirt.

"Mr. Thibodeaux?"

He nodded.

"Good afternoon. I'm Mrs. Jefferson, Madame Rousseau's housekeeper."

Oh-kay.

"Hi," he said.

"*Ms.* Rousseau—Jacqueline, that is—is in the gym. She asked that you meet her there."

Gardener took a deep breath, squinting around the entry hall that spanned twelve to fifteen feet in each direction. Cream blobs of wall bled into cream blobs of marble floor, and other than a blob of red in front of him, which he assumed from its shape was a staircase, he could barely make out anything else.

"Could you tell me where—"

"And she asked me to give you this," said Mrs. Jefferson, handing Gard an envelope.

He felt the telltale ridges of dollar bills inside, and his lips turned down. Wow. She was a piece of work, and he got the message loud and clear: she wouldn't be paying in Abita and kisses this time. Well, fine. Perfect. Better for everyone.

When he looked up, Mrs. Jefferson was gone, her footsteps far away.

Still holding the envelope, he stood in the large entryway, trying to get a bead on which direction Jax had gone last time, but he'd been so distracted by her getup, he'd followed her to the gym—ogling her ass—without keeping track of how she got there. Damn it. There were probably a hundred different doors in this massive atrium of an entryway—rooms, closets—and Lord only knew where he'd find the one that led downstairs. And shit, if he started opening random doors to find his way, he'd look like an idiot, not to mention he'd probably get lost.

"*Merde*," he muttered, taking several steps forward toward the red blob, finding that he was correct in assuming it was a grand staircase with red carpeting.

Grateful to discover he was right, he sat down on the steps, trying to figure out what to do. The front door was directly in front of him—he could tell by the bright light streaming in through the windows, even if he'd somehow gotten disoriented. He could start at the door, find the perimeter of the room and follow it around, opening every door as quietly as possible until he found the right one . . . or he could sit here on the steps and wait. Certainly Mrs. Jefferson would eventually walk by, or Jax, the duchess herself, would come looking for him. *After all*, he thought with a sneer, *she paid for my time*. Resting his elbows on his knees, he let the envelope fall from his fingers to the red-carpeted step beside him and let out a deep breath, thinking about his old life and missing it desperately.

This life, where he couldn't make his way through hedgerows or find his way downstairs in a house he'd already visited once before, made him feel like half a man, like a babe in the woods, when once upon a time, he'd been a protector. It was frustrating and humiliating, but the reality was that he was lucky to have the limited sight he had. He knew that. Some days he even tried to be grateful for it. It's just that he didn't know how to be both himself and also this—this shadow of who he used to be. But he had to figure it out or he'd go crazy, he'd—

"Gard? *Bon jour!*"

He hadn't heard her walk into the hallway, likely because she was barefoot, and her tan feet with chipped polish on the nails suddenly appeared directly in front of his sneakers, tiny in contrast.

"Here you are! I was wondering what—"

"I'm blind," he said softly, still staring at their feet.

"Wait. What?"

"I'm blind," he said again, looking up at her from where he sat on the steps, his heart thumping wildly behind his ribs as his pathetic truth tumbled from his lips. "I have no long distance vision and very little peripheral. The scars around my eyes . . ."

His voice trailed off and he sat in misery, letting his head fall forward with the shame of it. He should leave now. He should stand up and leave. She wouldn't stop him. She wouldn't come around anymore. She'd see how absurd it was for him to be teaching her self-defense, and he himself knew how absurd it was for him to be wanting things from her that she should only give to a man who could protect her and keep her safe. That's what she wanted, right? Right. And how could a blind man do any of that? He couldn't.

"I didn't know," she said, sitting down beside him.

"I'll go," he said, putting his hands flat on the step to stand up, but she stopped him, covering his hand with hers and pressing down.

"Why?"

"Why what?"

"Why are you going?"

He turned to face her, and because she was so close, he could see her clearly—her sweeping black lashes, gentle green eyes, and rosebud lips that he'd tasted over and over again in his daydreams since Monday. Her skin glistened with sweat and her cheeks were flushed from exercise.

"I just said I'm blind, Jax. Practically, anyway."

"I'm sorry," she said, slipping her fingers through his to anchor him beside her, "but I don't understand what that has to do with you teaching me some self-defense moves today like you promised."

He searched her eyes. "Why would you want a blind self-defense instructor?"

"First of all, you're not totally blind. I don't know how much of your eyesight is compromised, but it's definitely not all, because you make your way around. I've seen it. Second of all, you were a cop, weren't you?"

"Yes, but—"

"Which means you were trained to defend yourself."

"Duchess—"

"And you promised to teach me."

His face contorted with anger and frustration. "I couldn't even figure out how to get to your fuckin' basement! I'm as helpless as a goddamned kitten!"

She lifted her chin and took a deep breath, looking out at the hallway for several minutes before turning back to him and nailing him with a stern look, only tempered by a gentle tone.

"When you walk into this house through the middle set of doors, there is a another set to your left. Then a floor-to-ceiling window. Then a corner. A short bit of wall, then a door. That's the study we came through last time. Another bit of wall, then another door. That's a powder room, if you should ever need it. Another bit of wall, then a double opening. That leads to the formal living room, but skip it. It's dull as beige with lots of stupid Parisian knickknacks my mother kept from her ballerina days. After the double opening, there's a very small bit of wall and another door. Open it. Walk down the stairs. At the bottom, turn right. Walk down the hall. If you keep your hand on the wall to your right, you'll pass a screening room, then a studio. The third door on your right is the gym." She unlaced her fingers from his, though her smile was as sweet and warm as ever. "If you still want to train me today, I'll see you down there in ten minutes. If not, leave the envelope on the stairs, and I promise not to bother you ever again."

She stood up and stared down at him, and though he could make out her hands on her hips, from a distance of several feet above him, her features were a little hazier now.

"Someone recently told me," she said, "that building a life is about taking the pieces that matter and figuring out how to fit them together." She paused, her voice an emotional whisper when she added, "I hope I see you again."

His eyes burned and he blinked them rapidly, lowering his head as he listened to her retreating steps on the marble floor.

That's when he knew—as certainly as he'd ever known anything—that he was about to fall in love for the second time in his life. It didn't matter if they were ill-suited to one another, and it didn't matter in what condition they'd found each other. It didn't matter that he'd only known her for a handful of days or that she was rich and he was the neighbor's part-time gardener. It didn't matter that her French was Parisian and his was Cajun or that she was twenty-seven to his thirty-two. It didn't even matter that he had no plans for this love that had already started to take root inside of him. All that mattered was that in a moment when she could have done or said a million different things, Jacqueline Rousseau had somehow managed to choose a response that allowed him to keep his pride, his dignity, and his hope.

Oh Lord, he was going to fall.

And he was going to fall hard.

Unless he left Le Chateau right this minute and never looked back.

As soon as the hallway door closed behind her, Jax placed her palm over her heart and took a deep breath.

She'd suspected, of course, that something was wrong—he squinted all the time and had those scars around his eyes. Though she didn't know how he'd lost his sight, it made sense to her that he had, like puzzle pieces fitting correctly into place. He'd been blinded. No doubt on the job . . . which was why he wasn't a cop anymore.

She scrunched her eyes shut in pity for him, then opened them, lifted her chin, and quickly scurried down the stairs. She hadn't known Gard Thibodeaux long, but he was a proud man, and she was certain her pity would be unwelcome. Which is why she was so profoundly grateful she'd been able to temper her reaction and act with common sense when he'd told her.

Thank God for law school, she thought . . . and for living in the public eye for a short period of time. Hell, thank God for J.C.'s card-playing lessons the time they went to Monte Carlo for spring break. All had helped her achieve a pretty decent poker face, and it had certainly come in handy today. The look in his eyes when she'd said *I hope I see you again* was filled with such anguish, such longing, it made her chest clench.

Maybe she'd been wrong about that kiss after all. Maybe he had wanted it as much as she. Maybe the regret she'd picked up on had more to do with his situation than his feelings for her. Her heart leapt with stupid hope, and she told it to be still.

Turning at the bottom of the stairs, she walked briskly to the gym, beelined for the bathroom, and splashed some cold water on her face. She stared at her face in the mirror, willing him, with every cell in her body, to be waiting for her when she walked out. Over the past two days, while she'd been distracted by *Philadelphia Vice*, she'd missed him. It was ridiculous, sure, but she couldn't help it. Her infatuation with him wasn't going away. She could either try to ignore it or lean into it, and her stomach filled with butterflies as she realized he was about to make the decision for her. *Please let him be waiting outside when I open this door.* She'd be very sorry if today marked the end of their fledgling friendship and their deliciously hot flirtation. Jax wanted more from him—more time, more kisses—and damn it, but she'd *just* figured out a way to augment and extend their time together.

Please be waiting. Please.

Stepping out of the bathroom, she found him standing just inside the gym door, and she beamed with happiness, now knowing that he wouldn't be able to make out her expression from that distance. He hadn't left. She leaned in.

He squinted at her from across the room. "Jax?"

Toning down her megawatt smile, she crossed the room to stand before him. "Ready to get started?"

Looking into her eyes, he grinned—a different grin than she'd seen before. There was a warmth to it, an openness, a vulnerability that she hadn't seen yet, but she felt it everywhere. *Everywhere.* And her toes curled on the rubber floor.

He nodded slowly, checking her out from head to curled toes and making goose bumps spring up on her skin as he intoned in his low, dirty, Cajun-accented French, *"Oui, Duchesse. Laissez les bons temps rouler."*

Let the good times roll.

Her eyes flared with heat and her breath caught for a moment as she stood before him, and damn if he didn't feel all his blood rush south. He took a deep breath, but it was ragged and shallow in his ears, because he breathed her in—her warmth and her intoxicating scent. *Concentrate, Gard. Concentrate.* He had missed her, he was wildly attracted to her, and his feelings for her were growing by the second . . . but he had something important to say to her before they could actually get started with her next training session.

She licked her parted lips, her eyes dropping briefly to his mouth before sliding up again to meet his gaze.

Merde. She was going to kill him if she kept looking at him like that.

He held up the envelope between them. "I don't want this."

"It's what I owe you," she said. "It's fair."

"I'll train you, Jax," he said evenly, "but I'll train you for . . . six-packs of Abita."

Her lips twitched. "You want me to pay you in beer?"

And your company. It was on the tip of his tongue to say it, but at the last second, he simply nodded instead.

She shrugged, and a grin brightening her face. "I guess . . . friends do that sometimes?"

This time he nodded eagerly, his own smile sneaking out to join hers. "From what I hear, there aren't many rules between friends."

She chuckled at their inside joke. "Okay, then. Abita it is. I'll . . . head into town and grab some more."

"Come over tomorrow night?" he asked.

"Sure. I'll—oh, no. I can't tomorrow. I have plans."

Plans. *Shit.* Plans. The word fell like a brick tied around his heart. *With whom?* he wanted to ask—wanted to *demand*—but it was none of his business.

"Then whenever," he said dismissively, feeling stupid as he searched her eyes for clues about her mystery plans. Her emeralds sparkled ever so slightly, like she knew something funny that he didn't, and it made him scowl. "Let's . . . get started."

"With my siblings," she said gently, her shoulders shaking with giggles. "My brothers and sister. Family dinner. Thursday nights."

"Oh," he said, relief coursing through his veins like a tonic. "Oh. Good."

Her giggles stopped. Her eyes darkened.

"Anything else before we—?"

"Yeah. One more thing. It wasn't a blip, Duchess." He took a step closer to her. "It wasn't *just a kiss*. I don't know exactly what it was yet . . . but it wasn't nothin'."

He shrugged, leaving his thoughts there between them for her to accept or reject and hoping like hell for the former. She flinched for just a moment as if she pricked her finger on a needle, then offered him a wobbly smile.

"Good," she whispered. Her eyes were wide and warm, staring up at him with something that felt peculiarly like . . . open road.

He lifted his hand and placed his palm flush against the side of her throat and her eyelids fluttered closed. She leaned toward him, her body a breath away from his. And Lord, how he wanted to kiss her again, but if he did, he wouldn't end up teaching her a goddamned thing. And the thing is, he wanted her to learn. He needed to teach her how to protect herself so she'd be safe from assholes like Tripp.

"Today's lesson is about . . . the throat."

"The throat?" she squeaked, her eyes popping open.

"*Oui.* The throat," he said, his lips trembling as he tried not to smile at her.

"Tease," she muttered, frowning.

"You should know that *want* and *should* are having an epic battle in my head right now."

"Who's winning?" she asked.

"I *should* teach you how to protect yourself, *cher*."

Cher. Pronounced the Cajun "sha," the way his father said it to his mother so long ago. He didn't know where it had come from, but it sounded nice. It sounded right.

Her eyes softened for a moment, but then she took a deep breath and nodded. Her face sobered as she straightened her body away from his. "The throat. Let's go."

For the next hour, he taught her how to protect herself should she ever be grabbed from behind with a forearm under her throat. She practiced leaning her head forward as far as it would go, then using torque to slingshot it back and break her assailant's nose with the back of her head. He also taught her how to break free of a front chokehold by grabbing her assailant's wrists to pull him in close, then raising her knee to slam it into his balls. Except Jax, who was incredibly focused on the lesson, moved a bit too quick for him the third time around, proving that she'd perfected the move.

"Fuck!" he yelled, releasing his light grip on her throat and stumbling back as the pain of her assault shot through his groin, stealing his breath as his eyes filled with tears. It had been a long time since he'd taken a shot to the nuts, but glory Lord, it didn't hurt any less than he remembered.

"Oh my God!" she gasped. "Gard! Oh no! I'm so sorry!"

He put his hands on his knees and bent over, trying to catch his breath as lightning bolts of pain streaked through his entire pelvic region.

"I didn't mean to . . ."

"Good j-job," he wheezed.

"Are you okay?" she asked.

He looked up at her and slowly straightened, wincing from a fresh jolt of nausea. Shuffling to a chair by the door, he sat down gingerly with only the very back of one ass cheek resting on the seat.

"Do you need ice?" she asked, standing in front of him, wringing her hands together.

"You just killed my future children," he groaned.

"I'm sorry," she said softly. "I feel terrible."

"Not as terrible as I feel, Duchess."

"What can I do?"

"Distract me."

"O-okay," she said. "Okay. I, um, I have an idea. Want to hear it?"

"Does it include you takin' off your sports bra?"

She shook her head no, but her emeralds sparkled just the way he liked.

"Go 'head," he said, nodding weakly.

"I looked through the scripts. After we talked on Monday? I looked through them."

He had no idea where she was going with this. "Okay. And?"

"I found one. A good one, I think. But it's not a movie. It's TV."

"What's the . . . difference?" he asked, the last part coming out in a groan as the pain lessened from white-hot intensity to a throbbing ache.

She shrugged. "I don't know all the differences yet."

"Go on."

"It's, um, well, it's a police procedural called *Philadelphia Vice*, and I—"

"Like *CSI*?"

"More like *Law and Order*."

This was interesting. "Based on the Philly PD?"

She nodded.

Unbelievably, her nonnaked distraction was actually helping. The nausea was subsiding and he could sit back a little. "Go on."

"I was wondering . . . that is, if you had the time . . ."

"You want me to take a look at it? At the script?"

She shrugged, but her sweet lips had already tilted up into a little smile. "Would you?"

"Why not? I'll take it with me and look at it tonight. I can still read, thank God."

"Thank you!" she said, leaning forward like she was going to hug him, then wincing and taking a step back. "That means a lot to me. It's the first project I've been excited about in months."

"In that case, I'll do you one better, *Duchesse*," he said, finally standing up again. "Want to see a real cop hangout? Best way to know if your scriptwriter is capturing the real thing."

"Are you serious?" Her eyes widened. "Yeah! I mean, yes! I'd love it."

"Friday night?"

"Sure! Yes!" she said.

"One catch, though," he said, taking a deep breath and hating what he had to say next. But if he was going to figure out how to live this life, he had to start somewhere. "I can't drive anymore."

Her smile was blinding. "Good thing I can."

Exhaling with relief as he stared at her lips, he actually *felt* himself start to fall, and instead of scowling, he smiled back at her, because there wasn't one goddamn thing he cared to do about it.

Chapter 9

Last night, Jax had enjoyed one of Mad's signature dinners—blue cheese, fig, prosciutto, and arugula pizza with a fresh herb salad and homemade orange sorbet for dessert. Everything fresh. Everything delicious, of course.

As they sat down for dinner, Mad casually asked about Gard, and Jax's expression alone was enough to let the cat out of the bag.

"Oh. My. God!" exclaimed Mad as Jax's cheeks flushed. "Did you sleep with him?"

"Way to go, Jax," said J.C., waging war with a difficult wine cork. "I would've thought there were cobwebs down there by now."

"You're disgusting," she told her brother, who wedged the wine bottle between his thighs and kept pulling. "I hope you end up with Merlot on your jeans."

"Shut up, Jean-Christian," said Mad. She turned to Jax. "Tell me what's going on!"

"It was . . ." She was about to say "nothing," but she could hear his voice in her head saying, *I don't know exactly what it was yet . . . but it wasn't nothin'*, and she couldn't. "We kissed."

Mad gasped. "And . . . ?"

Jax grinned, then rolled her eyes. "It was a good kiss."

"Who is this guy again?" asked J.C., finally wrestling the cork out of the bottle with a satisfying pop.

"The Englishes' gardener," supplied Mad, holding out her glass.

"Huh. Slumming?" asked J.C., pouring a healthy splash for Mad.

"What?" Jax gave him a look. "No. No! He's just . . . he's teaching me self-defense."

"And tonsil hockey," said J.C., pouring Jax a glass. "Someone's cavorting with the help."

"Shut up, J.C. You're a horse's ass."

"*I'm* an ass? What would our *chère maman* say about you fucking the neighbor's gardener?" he asked with a smirk.

Jax's eyes narrowed. "I'm *not* fucking him, one. And two . . . who cares? She's in Paris."

"Well, he's certainly not the right kind. Kate English is the *right* kind," J.C. reminded her, "and *Maman* barely tolerates her."

"Well, in case you hadn't noticed," said Jax. "I'm an adult. I'll screw whomever I please. Not that I am. I mean, *we're* not. I just . . . I like him." She shrugged, peeking at Mad over her wine glass. "And I'm reading scripts again."

"You are?" asked Mad, her smile dreamy and happy. "Then I like him too."

"Long live Queen Jax and the lowly gardener," said J.C., raising his glass to her, then snickering. Just as he raised his glass to his lips, Jax kicked his shin under the table and a big splash of Merlot soaked his pink-and-white pinstripe dress shirt. "*Merde!* You little bitch!"

"Stop being an asshole," said Jax, raising an eyebrow. "And don't tell mother."

She didn't actually need to say it. She already knew they wouldn't. Neither Mad nor J.C. would say a word—the Rousseau children had bonded over their absentee parents years ago, and their union as siblings was much stronger than the relationship any of them held individually with Liliane.

Anyway, Jax had no idea what would happen with Gardener, though she'd liked it very much when he had told her that their kiss wasn't a "blip" or "just a kiss." Like him, she didn't know where they were going or where that sweet kiss would lead. But also like him, she knew in her heart that it wasn't insignificant, and it was like a precious, sweet secret to know they both felt that way.

She had gone to sleep last night thinking about tonight— how she would pick him up at eight and drive them both into the city, to a bar near his old precinct. He told her, "the fries are greasy, but the beer is cold. Think you can handle it, Duchess?" She'd asked if they'd be meeting some of his friends, and he said they'd likely run into some people he knew. What she wondered the most, as she drifted off to sleep, was how he'd introduce her tomorrow. As his friend? As more? What *was* she to him? Oh, she knew it was too soon to put labels on the newness of their *petite romance*, but it made her feel excited to wonder, so she thought about it all the same.

This morning, she'd forced herself not to daydream about her date anymore and spent a couple of hours checking out "Sailing-Themed Movie Parties" on Pinterest, where she discovered some awesome ideas to share with Skye. Over the last few days, her excitement for Skye's party had doubled and tripled, and a possible new life had started taking shape in Jax's head: it included making her home at Le Chateau, seeking out friendships with women like Skye and Daisy, and producing a television program filmed on-site in Philadelphia. The more she thought about it, the more right it felt, though the pieces weren't laid out just so and ready to be snapped together.

First and foremost, Le Chateau didn't belong to her. It belonged to her mother. She would have to buy it from her mother to officially make it hers. Though it hadn't been appraised in ages, Jax guessed the house was worth around seven million dollars, and while she could certainly buy it outright from her trust, it would deplete the trust by about a quarter after taxes were paid. Still, she *could* afford it. But common sense asked why a single woman required a seven-million-dollar, six-acre, eight-bedroom, twelve-bathroom estate with a grand ballroom, swimming pool, gym, studio, and theater. For a family of six, it had been ostentatious. For her? By herself? It bordered on ridiculous. Not to mention that her mother was mercurial—there was no guarantee that Liliane would sell it to Jax. She didn't like the house and never had. It wouldn't surprise Jax if she was eager to be rid of it once and for all.

And while she was hopeful that Skye and Daisy were potential friends, especially after today's luncheon, the reality was that both women had been raised in working-class families, while Jax had been raised on Blueberry Lane. Would their sensibilities about life bwe vastly different? Would the three women be able to connect, or would Skye and Daisy see Jax as an entitled trust-fund brat who had taken a life of luxury for granted? Or worse, would they see her as a big-shot Hollywood producer whose life felt too removed from theirs to see her as a friend? Could she convince them that she was also just a down-to-earth girl who was thinking about relocating and needed friends just as much as anyone else?

And what *about* producing a TV series on location in Philadelphia so she could make her home here, where she had friends and family and felt safe? It wasn't like a movie: a big one-time project that had a beginning, middle, and end. It was more like a job—an ongoing gig that could last for years if the show found an audience. Not to mention, would her success as a Hollywood producer even translate to the small screen? Or would she be laughed at for trying something new?

With these thoughts weighing on her mind, she slipped through the hedgerow from Le Chateau to Westerly and took a deep breath, deciding that for today—just for now— she would just worry about connecting with Skye and Daisy and tackle the rest later.

"Jax! Hello!" called Skye from the back patio, waving her over to an elegant lunch table.

"Hi!" said Jax, smiling at Skye as she hopped up the steps, and offering her hostess a massive bouquet of wildflowers. "I brought flowers."

"My God! A whole greenhouse of them!"

"Too much?" asked Jax, cringing as Skye cradled the bouquet in her arms.

"Only if I hated flowers. Which I don't!" The maid hurried out from the house and Skye turned to her. "Fran, can you find a—a . . ."

"A vase, ma'am?"

Skye nodded. "Yes, a vase. Can you find one for these?"

Fran took the flowers and headed back into the house as Skye turned to Jax and gestured for her to take a seat. Her cheeks had pinkened. "My—that is, my mother wasn't around much when I was little. Or . . . ever, really. I didn't grow up with many flowers to put in vases."

"My mother wasn't around much either," said Jax, hoping her confession would place Skye at more ease.

"Oh. Were your parents . . . divorced?"

"No. Just absent." Jax reached into her purse for her sunglasses and put them on. "Mostly traveling the world for business. Or pleasure. Or just to be away together. Or just to be away from us."

"They loved each other?" asked Skye.

Jax nodded. "I think so. Certainly more than they loved us."

Skye sighed. "Well, I think we both turned out great."

"You barely know me," said Jax, reaching for her wine glass.

"I know you're nice. And funny. You made a great movie." Skye took a sip of her wine. "Besides, Brooks said you're a 'good egg.'"

Jax lowered her glass, grinning. She'd never been very close to Brooks, so his compliment surprised her and delighted her at once. "He did?"

She nodded. "Yes. He said to steer clear of your brother, a couple of the Story sisters, and Sloane Ambler. But he said you were solid."

"Steer clear of J.C.?" she asked, grinning.

"Yes."

Jax nodded her agreement. "Brooks has a point. He's a terrible flirt."

Skye gave her a wide-eyed nod. "So I've heard."

They were both giggling as Fran opened the door to the terrace and a beautiful blonde woman walked onto the patio with a cellophane-covered basket hanging from her arm. She was Daisy English, wife of the second-oldest English brother, Fitz.

"Hey, girls!" she called, heading to the table and pulling out the available chair. "What did I miss?"

"Daisy!" greeted Skye, standing to embrace her friend. "So good to see you . . . without spit-up on my shoulder."

"Or a diaper bag filled to bursting," said Daisy, turning to grin at Jax. "Hey, Jax."

"Hi, Daisy. It's good to see you," said Jax, reaching her hand across the table to shake Daisy's.

Daisy glanced at Skye, then back at Jax. "We do a Mommy and Me class together at Enchanted Beginnings in Wayne on Wednesday mornings."

"But aren't your children pretty different in age?" asked Jax. She'd seen Daisy and Fitz's daughter at Étienne and Kate's wedding, and she looked a *lot* bigger than tiny Sailor.

Skye shrugged. "Sailor's two months and Caroline will be a year old in . . . ?"

"July," said Daisy.

"Well, there you go. The class is for babies twelve months and under."

"Enough about kids!" exclaimed Daisy suddenly, taking her seat. "Today I'm just a grown-up, drinking wine with lunch and talking about *anything* but organic puff snacks and the 'right' preschool!"

"Amen," said Skye, raising her glass. "The terror is fast asleep, which means I have two hours to get you two drunk, hear your secrets, and plan a party!"

Jax lifted her glass and giggled. "To wine, secrets, and parties!"

They clanked the crystal glasses together, and each took a long sip of ice-cold Chardonnay.

Daisy sighed as she replaced her glass. "Starting to feel human again."

"Jax," said Skye as Fran returned with warm rolls and plated salad, "remind us of what it's like out there."

"In the dating world?" asked Jax. She took another sip of wine. "Probably less glamorous than you remember."

Daisy shook her head. "Actually, I remember it being pretty awful."

Skye shrugged. "My boyfriend before Brooks was *such* an asshole."

"I didn't even *have* a boyfriend before Fitz," said Daisy. "Just a fake one to make him jealous."

"Did it work?" asked Jax, chuckling as she buttered her roll.

Daisy nodded, flashing her rock of a diamond ring at Jax. "Sure did."

"How did you . . ." She paused, thinking of Gard's words on Wednesday afternoon: *It wasn't just a kiss. I don't know exactly what it was yet . . . but it wasn't nothin'.* "How did you know that Brooks . . . or Fitz . . . was the one?"

Skye sipped her wine, her expression going dreamy. "We were from totally different worlds, you know? Me, a boat mechanic. Him, an Olympic millionaire."

"Us too," said Daisy. "I baked cookies for a living out in Oregon and lived in a studio apartment." She looked over at Haverford Park meaningfully. "He is . . . Fitz English."

Jax nodded, leaning closer, thinking that she and Gard were from two different worlds too. If it worked out for Daisy and Fitz, and Skye and Brooks, maybe, just maybe—

"The first kiss," said Skye, closing her eyes for just a moment. When she opened them, she licked her lips and raised her wine glass to her mouth. "It was . . ."

"Electric," said Daisy. "And I'm not even counting the teenage kisses. I'm only counting the one when we found each other again. The back hallway of Mulligan's. Oh my God, I thought I'd go up in flames right there."

"Mulligan's, the bar? At UPenn?" asked Jax.

Daisy nodded. "That's the one. There's an old phone closet in the back."

"I was still with my ex the first time we kissed," confessed Skye, spearing a lettuce leaf covered with parmesan cheese. "Brooks apologized to me. Told me it would never happen again, but . . ."

"You were already ruined," whispered Jax, on the edge of her seat.

Skye paused midbite, her smart, clear-blue eyes scanning Jax's face. "Yeah. Something like that."

Daisy and Skye exchanged a look, then Daisy asked in an overly casual tone, "Do you have a boyfriend, Jax?"

"No."

"But there's someone," said Skye knowingly.

"And I'm betting a *new* someone," said Daisy.

"I don't know." Jax picked up her wine glass and took a small sip. "Maybe."

"You have to tell us!" said Daisy.

"No way," said Jax, feeling her cheeks flush. "Not until there's something, you know, to tell. And anyway, we're here to talk about Skye's party!"

Both women stared at her without flinching.

Daisy broke first. "We'll promise to drop it if you promise to bring him."

"Bring him?"

"Yes. We won't ask you any more about him, but if he's still in the picture in a few more weeks," said Skye, in total collusion with her Mommy and Me friend, "bring him to the party."

Bring the gardener, Gardener, to a party at Westerly.

Bring the gardener, who was a son of a gardener, to a party on Blueberry Lane.

Bring the gardener to a party his employers' sons would be attending.

Bring the gardener, of whom her mother would never, ever approve, to a party with the Winslows, Englishes, Storys, and Amblers.

Bring him.

She took a long sip of wine, and when she finally lowered her glass, she grinned at her new friends. "Deal."

"Wonderful," said Skye. "Now let's talk about my party!"

After they'd hammered out the party details, they'd sat in the sun for another hour laughing and talking, and Jax was surprised and gratified by how easily she'd slipped into a comfortable rapport with the other two women.

They were all right around the same age, and even though Daisy and Skye were married with young children, Jax had felt totally at ease with them, talking about TV shows they all loved and books they'd recently read. And as an hour turned into two and the first wine bottle was quickly traded for another, Jax realized that there was a lot to like about these suburban moms raising their children in safe, lovely Haverford and its environs. Before now, she hadn't felt strong pangs for marriage and children, but as she walked back to Le Chateau after agreeing to go to Daisy's house for another "planning" lunch the Friday after next, she felt them for the first time in her life.

A warm home. Children. A man who loved her. So much to love about the lives that Daisy and Skye were living.

And Jax would do it all differently—so differently from the way her parents had done it. She'd be a hands-on mom, like Skye and Daisy, taking Mommy and Me classes with her babies and spending time with them on purpose—because she wanted to. She wouldn't foist them off on a nanny before they were able to speak, and she wouldn't jet off to Paris, or Los Angeles, or Tokyo and hire a paid nurse when one (or four) of them came down with the chicken pox. She would spend long summer days running through the sprinkler with them and teaching them how to swim. She would tuck them in at night, telling them "*Vous etes si belle que vous regarder est une souffrance*" after singing them lullabies in French and pushing their dirty-blond hair from their foreheads—

"Wait!" she exclaimed, stopping in her tracks. She blinked twice, turning to look over her shoulder, not at Westerly, but at the chimneys of Haverford Park just beyond, where a dirty-blond-haired gardener would be waiting for her in just a few hours.

"No, no, no, no, no," she said, quickening her pace as she ducked through the hedgerow. "You barely know him!"

And yet the image was there in her head. As clear as day. A sleeping child with the gardener's hair, falling asleep to lullabies sung in soft and dirty French.

If Gardener Thibodeaux had ever believed that only women got the jitters before a first date, the way he'd felt all day would have soundly trounced such an idiotic notion. As he pulled an old border of pachysandra from around the swimming pool area, he thought of nothing but Jax.

It wasn't that he was nervous about spending time with her . . . since meeting her, he *craved* time with her, and not seeing her since Wednesday afternoon's lesson had felt like a long time.

It wasn't that he was nervous about taking her to Club7, the restaurant and bar associated with the Philadelphia Brotherhood of Police. He was proud to be seen with Jax Rousseau. If he ran into the guys he used to work with, they'd be blown away by the girl on his arm.

That said, he wasn't entirely sure she was ready to see the guys he used to work with. He hadn't been around them much since Gil's death and his own retirement. Several of his buddies had tried to reach out to him, but he'd ignored their attempts. What if he ran into them tonight? And what if they talked about what had happened in any detail? Did he owe it to Jax to fill her in first?

Speaking of Jax, it felt really weird and really wrong to have her pick him up and drive them. But the thing was, he needed to figure out how to live *this* life. And living this life meant letting other people drive sometimes. Sure, he could have rented a limo and driver, but that wasn't him. That wasn't who he was. Trying to find a silver lining, he reminded himself that even if she was driving, he still got to be alone with her.

Over the past two days, he'd read her script, and while he'd found it lacking in some realism, overall he thought it was a strong project. It was the story of a multigenerational cop family with Irish roots, and the protagonist, a third-generation female cop named Jenny O'Laughlin, starts her first day as a vice detective when the series begins. Though she's been led to believe that she'll be conducting investigations, instead she's asked about her willingness to go undercover as a prostitute in a long-term sting.

The series, which would explore the underbelly of Philadelphia's prostitution and narcotics rings by way of a department insider, could be a fascinating study of the "other side" of vice, flush with opportunities for drama in Jenny's job, with her family, and with her boyfriend, a fireman who won't find out what she's been doing until episode five or six.

Gard could understand why Jax had liked it, and he knew plenty of cops with whom she could speak, to be sure she got the script perfect every time. Heck, *he* could work with her as an advisor, tweaking a word here and there, correcting a misconception, or just keeping the show as accurate as possible. Even though he'd worked SVU, he could still—

No.

No, he couldn't.

He sighed, gathering a pile of pachysandra, throwing it into a wheelbarrow, and heading back toward the gardening shed.

More than once over the last few days, he'd gotten carried away like this. The script was compelling enough to make him dream about having a chance to put all his now-worthless knowledge to good use once again. But he needed to remind himself that life was gone. He wasn't a cop anymore. He wasn't a TV script advisor. He was a gardener, and if he didn't want any more disappointment in his life, he'd do well to remember it.

After dropping off the wheelbarrow, he headed back to his apartment and took a shower, soaping his body and shampooing his hair. Watching as the water finally ran clear, he shifted his mind back to Jax, trying to figure out what the hell was going on between them and wishing he had the willpower to walk away now instead of watching her walk away later.

But instead of coming up with a plan of defense, as would be prudent, more and more he felt himself leaning into whatever was happening between them. His heart, which had been brutalized by Tiffany years ago, had recovered and was strong enough to fall in love again. And no matter how much of a bad choice Jax Rousseau seemed to be in theory, his head and his heart (and his dick, for Lord's sake) wouldn't admit it.

He liked her.

He liked her a lot.

And as far as he could tell, the whole game of "Did she or didn't she?" was over. She liked him too. He was certain of it.

So he'd sort of tacitly decided that without taking advantage of her or pressuring her, he'd take what he could get . . . and when it was over—when she returned to Hollywood or New York or wherever her bold and glamorous destiny would take her—he would have an eternity to get over her. For now? He just wanted to enjoy her. He'd endured two years of hell; he'd earned a little bit of heaven.

After shaving and running a brush through his thick dark-blond hair, he stepped naked into his bedroom and tugged on a clean pair of jeans, a white T-shirt, and a white button-down shirt, which he rolled up at the cuffs and tucked into the jeans. Pulling his pewter medal of St. Michael, the patron saint of cops, from his dresser drawer, he put it around his neck for the first time in over a year, slipping it beneath his T-shirt and whispering part of the policemen's prayer—"Give me a cool head and a stout heart . . ."—as he slid his feet into black loafers and grabbed a black leather belt from his closet doorknob.

As he threaded the belt through the loops of denim, he thought about having a drink to calm his nerves but chastised himself as a fucking coward for the idea. Grabbing his keys from a hook by the door, he pulled it shut behind him and headed for the gates of Haverford Park to wait for her.

Jax pulled up in front of the Englishes' estate, unsurprised to see Gard standing by the front pillars, his body tall, masculine, and graceful in jeans and a white shirt. What did surprise her, however, was her reaction to him.

Her heart instantly sped up.

Her breathing quickened.

Her skin flushed.

Her toes curled.

She sighed.

Merde but she had it bad for this man.

He approached her Mercedes S-Class sedan, whistling low as he opened the door and swung his body into the passenger seat.

"*Bon soir, Duchesse,*" he said, grinning at her.

"Hi," she said, ridiculously happy to be around him again.

"There have been many times I wished I could get behind the wheel of a car again, but none of those moments made me want to cry as much as this one," he said, reaching out to caress the dashboard before him. He slid his glance back to her. "This is one fine automobile, Jax Rousseau."

"It's not mine," she said, butterflies filling her tummy. "It belongs to my mother. I'm just borrowing it."

She watched as he reached for his seatbelt and buckled himself in, the dark-blond hair on his tan forearm golden in the light of the setting sun. His arms were strong and muscular, corded with veins and muscle. Manly hands. Rough hands that would chafe her soft skin if he touched her. As if her thought could influence the movement of his hand, it suddenly rose, the backs of his fingers stopping when he reached her chin, resting there for a moment before gently lifting her face and forcing her eyes to meet his.

"Hi," he said.

"Hi."

"You look beautiful tonight."

"Thank you."

"You smell like lemons and rosemary."

"Is that . . . ?"

". . . okay?" he said softly. "I love it."

"Good," she whispered, mesmerized by the closeness of him, longing for more from him.

"Listen, now." He drew closer to her, his chest leaning over the bolster between them, his drawl low and serious when he spoke again. "I'm goin' to kiss you, Duchess. And this time, it's not goin' to be a blip or a mistake or *just* a kiss. Got it?"

His eyes, almost black and wide with hunger, searched hers for a refusal, but he wouldn't find any. She'd been dreaming of this moment for two straight days.

Raising her hands, she cupped his jaw and pulled him closer, her breath jagged with anticipation and need. "Got it."

His lips weren't gentle and tentative this time. They crashed down on hers, urgent, impatient, and greedy, his fingers plunging into her hair and tilting her head to the side so that he could seal his mouth over hers. She moaned, her fingers clutching at his face as his tongue licked the seam of their lips and slipped into her mouth. She arched forward, meeting the touch of his tongue, tasting, twisting, swallowing the low groan that rose from his throat and was offered to her in surrender. Nibbling her lips, he tilted his head the other way, then kissed her again. Her breasts strained, aching for the firm pressure of his chest pressed flush against her throbbing nipples.

But the bolster. The goddamned bolster wasn't going to let it happen.

She whimpered with frustration, pulling away and looking up at him—at his midnight-black eyes and slick lips. His chest rose and fell rapidly with his breathing, and she couldn't look away, panting in time with him as he stared back at her.

"Glad we got that straightened out," he said, his eyes fierce, his body taut. He slowly pulled his hands from her hair and cupped her cheeks, his gaze drinking her in for a thirst he couldn't seem to quench.

She smiled at him—a tender, relieved grin accompanied by a wistful whimper. "Should we—maybe we should stay in tonight? We could watch a movie or . . ."

. . . make out for hours.

He leaned forward and touched his lips to hers again. "I promised you greasy fries and cold beer. Besides, don't you want to know what I think about your script?"

Her eyes flared open, all her blissed-out dreaminess taking flight. The project! Wow, he'd distracted her so much, she'd almost forgotten!

"Yes! I mean, yes, I'm dying to know what you thought!"

Sliding his hands from her face, he punched the address of Club7 into her GPS, then leaned back into the supple leather and smiled at her. "Then let's get out of here." Lowering his voice as she pulled onto Blueberry Lane, he added meaningfully, "We'll stay in another night, Duchess. I promise."

A delicious shiver sailed down Jax's spine as she put the car into reverse to turn around and head into the city.

Chapter 10

It was a forty-five-minute drive from Haverford to Northeast Philadelphia where Club7 was located, which would give Gard more than enough time to talk to her about her script. But first, he'd decided to tell her about what had happened on that fateful day two years ago. He took a deep breath and let it go slowly, forcing himself to stay calm as he prepared to recount the details of the worst day of his life.

"Jax," he started, as she merged onto the highway, "I gotta tell you a little more about my eyes. Could come up tonight if we run into someone I know. I'd rather you . . . you know, hear it from me."

She glanced over at him in surprise, but her voice was gentle. "Okay."

He looked away from her, concentrating on the broken white lines on either side of the highway lane. "Two years ago, my partner and I were called to the scene of a domestic abuse situation. Mother and two children livin' with her brother, who was high on meth and wieldin' a loaded weapon." He looked over at her and noted the set of her face—deep in concentration, no judgment, no repulsion. He continued. "My partner, Gil, he knocked on the door. We had our firearms cocked and ready. But when Miguel Santiago opened the door holdin' a rifle, he was—he was hopped up and paranoid, and he discharged his shotgun immediately. Gil's face was mostly blown off by the blast. Mine took a good bit of birdshot to the upper half."

She gasped, wincing as her right hand released the steering wheel and reached blindly for him. He caught her fingers between his, lacing them together, holding on tight.

"Go on," she said in a small, breathy voice.

"Paramedics tried to save Gil, but he died an hour later after endurin' so much pain, it makes me . . . makes me . . ." He blinked against the sudden burn in his eyes, but her fingers squeezed his, giving him the strength to finish. He shook his head and sighed. "Ahhh. Anyway, I—I was relatively lucky by comparison. The skin of my face was peppered with shot, but somehow, by some miracle, I only got one pellet in my left eye and two in my right. They were able to remove them." He gulped, flinching at the memory of his eyes on fire, his face filled with tiny lead pellets, the scalpel and tweezers plucking them out until the drugs kicked in and he passed out from the intense pain and welcome relief. There were still some pellets of birdshot there, lodged in bone or too deep in the muscle to get at. He'd have them forever. "But they did a lot of damage. Lot of damage. Even after several surgeries, they weren't able to restore my vision. Ophthalmologist said he'd go another two or three rounds, but he was honest with me—it was a matter of degrees at this point. I'd maybe get a slight bit of the peripheral back or—or some slight measure of the distance. Not enough to matter. I called uncle. I'd had enough."

She took a deep breath and held it a moment before he heard her release it. When she spoke, he could tell that she was trying hard not to cry. "What . . . um, I mean, where were you living during that time?"

"Here. In Philly." He shook his head. "I took early retirement and disability. Blind man ain't much good to the force."

"And who was—I mean, who was looking after you?"

"*I* was lookin' after me," he said, rubbing the pad of his thumb over the softness of the skin on the back of her hand.

"You were all alone?"

Gard looked out the window and sighed, shaking his head. His voice held an edge of warning he couldn't help. "Don't pity me, Jax."

She cleared her throat and lifted her chin. "I don't. I'm just mad at your mother and sisters."

Looking back over at her, he chuckled with surprise. "Is that right?"

"Yes!" she exclaimed. "They couldn't come up and give you a hand? Take care of you?"

"I could still walk and talk, *cher*."

"But you couldn't *see*. You couldn't *drive*. And you were in *pain*. I would've . . . I would've . . ."

"What would you have done, Jax?"

"I would have been here. I would have taken care of you!"

His stomach flipped over and he held the breath in his lungs, the fierce promise of her words affecting him more deeply than she could ever imagine. She was kind and loyal, strong and good. She was a fucking work of art, this woman. And for tonight, at the very least, she was with him.

Finally he exhaled, concentrating to keep his voice even. "I didn't want them here playing nursemaid. I did okay on my own."

"With bandages covering your eyes? And constant doctors' appointments? You lost your partner. You lost your job. You were *shot in the face*. Oh! I could scream!"

"Take a breath, Duchess. It's okay," he said, adjusting their fingers to hold hers tighter. "I wasn't all alone. Gil's sister, Mary, kept an eye on me. Drove me around. Took me to the hospital. Bought me groceries."

"Oh," said Jax, flicking a sour glance at him. "How kind."

Gard nodded. "Yes, she is."

"Is?"

"Alive and well."

"His *married* sister?"

"Very *un*married," said Gard, guiltily loving every bit of her jealousy. But *merde,* it was hot as hell.

"She spent a *lot* of time helping you?"

"She did."

"Morning, noon, and . . . night, I guess."

"You guess right, Duchess."

She wrangled her fingers from his, clamping them around the wheel. "Well, thank goodness for sister Mary," she muttered, fuming.

"*Mon dieu!* Do you know her too?"

"Know her? No!"

"Because that's exactly what I call her. Sister Mary. Because, you know, she's a nun."

"W-What?" She shot him a quick look before sliding her eyes back to the highway. Her lips twitched, though she tried to stop them from turning up into a smile. "You're a jerk."

He reached for her hand, gently prying it away from the wheel and drawing it to his lips. Kissing the soft skin gently, he murmured, "Aw, Duchess, if you saw the way your emeralds flash when you get a little jealous? Glory Lord, you'd understand. You'd even forgive me."

She didn't look at him, but her tongue darted out to lick her lips and she didn't pull her hand away. "My . . . emeralds?"

"Your eyes. *Tes yeux, j'en reve jour et nuit.*"

I dream of your eyes day and night.

His crush on her was making him goddamned cheesy. But Jax? His duchess? She didn't seem to mind a bit. Her cheeks pinkened and she razed her bottom lip with her teeth.

He opened her hand and pressed his lips to her palm. "Do that again and I'll make you pull over so I can kiss you again."

"We're on the highway," she gasped, darting him a wide-eyed look.

"I don't care."

"You're distracting me," she said, shaking her head, a smile playing at the corners of her lips.

"Good." *Except, also . . . not good.* She was driving, and he'd never forgive himself if he was teasing her and she got into an accident. He placed her hand back on the steering wheel and sat back in his seat. "We should talk about your script."

"Good. Yes. What did you think?" she asked, her voice tentative.

"It has a lot of promise."

"You think?"

"Absolutely."

"You liked it?"

"Yes, I did. I think the premise is solid. I know a ton of third-generation cops, and a lot of them are Irish. The twist of her showin' up for work the first day and bein' asked to go undercover is great. How's she goin' to sidestep turnin' tricks? How's she goin' to get the girls and johns to trust her? How's she goin' to stay safe? Great questions. And her father was a department chief back in the day. Fantastic. He's goin' to have real mixed feelin's about the way she's doin' her job. Not to mention her boyfriend's a firefighter. He's goin' to be real pleased to find out what his woman's doin' every day . . . or night. There's a lot goin' on. It's good, Jax. Real good."

"So you think I should pursue it?"

He shrugged. "I mean, I'm an ex-cop turned part-time gardener, so what do I know about Hollywood and TV? But yeah, I was certainly entertained."

"You're . . . what? Thirty?"

"Thirty-two."

"Thirty-two-year-old college-educated male. Gard, you're our target market. If you're entertained, that means something to me."

"Tricky filmin' it out there," he said, referring to California and purposely reminding himself that she'd be going back to Hollywood someday to make her TV show and he'd be left behind. It hurt to think about it, but he needed to be realistic about their time together.

"On the streets?" she asked. "Yeah, I guess. I'll need to have the production staff look into permits and all. But a lot of the filming would take place at night, I'm thinking. Probably easier to get it approved."

"You'll have to be careful with the sets. You know, to keep it authentic."

She nodded, flicking a grin at him. "Maybe we can take a field trip to some of the more authentic neighborhoods? You know, a little scouting trip? For inspiration?"

Those emeralds sparkled as she glanced over at him, an excited smile brightening her beautiful face. He felt it deep inside, in that place where sacred things are realized, that he'd do just about anything to see her shine.

"Whatever you want, Duchess," he said.

For as long as I've got you . . . anything *you want.*

Tucked protectively into Gard's side, with his arm around her shoulders, Jax watched his one-time coworkers rally around him, telling stories about his time on the force. They'd been at Club7 for an hour, and though he'd made good on the promise to buy her a cold beer or two, they still hadn't managed to sit down at a table. Every time they moved an inch toward the dining room, it seemed liked five more guys appeared, all wanting to buy Gard drinks, tell him how good he was looking, and gab about the old days.

Being Jax Rousseau in Hollywood had nothing on being Gardener Thibodeaux at Club7. That was for sure.

It seemed he was universally liked and respected, with cops and detectives from all units of the police department swinging by the gleaming mahogany bar to buy him a drink and welcome him back to the fold.

"Where you been, Gard?" asked Johnny Sanders, whom Gard had introduced to her a moment before.

Johnny's partner, Phil, chimed in. "Gil and Gard. Gard and Gil. Hear about you two all the time. You were a couple of badass motherfuckers."

"Hey," said Gard, squeezing Jax's shoulder. "Lady present, huh?"

"Yeah, right. Sorry, miss." Phil took a second look at Jax and grinned. "What the heck you doing with this old-timer anyway?"

"Old-timer!" whooped Frankie D., whom Gard had introduced as a fellow detective. Frankie elbowed the gray-haired man, Saul, who stood beside him. "You hear that, Saulie? Gard's an old-timer. Guess we've got one foot in the grave!"

"Know what I miss about Gard?" asked Saul, winking at Jax.

"No," she said, "but I'd love to know."

"Come on, Frankie. You know what I'm about to say!"

Frankie nodded, then cupped his hands around his mouth. "GUMBO NIGHT!"

All four men laughed, raising their beer glasses to toast.

"To gumbo," said Saul. "May it pass through our lips again!"

"Sooner than later!"

Gard lifted his glass in cheers, then they all finished off whatever was left of their beers, slamming their pint glasses down on the bar as Phil ordered another round.

From behind them, Jax heard a slurred voice ask, "Did I hear someone talking about gumbo night?"

While the other four men drinking with them were still laughing and reminiscing among themselves, Jax felt Gard tense beside her, his whole body—every muscle she could feel—flexed, tightening, ready to pounce.

"Brad," said Gard softly—the sound a curse, a swear—as the man rounded the group and came into view. He was overweight, his belly hanging over the lip of his navy-blue pants, and he had some beer suds clinging to his mustache. He looked harmless, laughable even. But Jax glanced up at Gard, watching his face harden, his lips tightening into a thin slash.

"Gardener Thibodeaux," said the man in an exaggerated Southern drawl, giving Gard a shit-eating grin. "What y'all doin' back here at Club7, honey child?"

Jax shifted her glance to Frankie D., who gave her what appeared to be a sympathetic grimace before asking the bartender for a cup of strong black coffee.

She looked back at Brad, who flicked his glance to Jax, his eyebrows riding up with appreciation as he licked his slick lips, leaning toward her. A little of his beer sloshed onto her shoes. "Aren't you going to introduce me?"

Gard's voice was lethal. "No."

"Still holding a grudge, huh?" asked the older man, smirking at Gard.

Saul put a hand on Gard's shoulder. "Remember, son," he said in a low voice, "fighting gets you banned."

Gard's head jerked slightly, an action of acknowledgment for Saul as he stared back at Brad with utter hatred.

"Hey, Brad," said Johnny, putting his arm around Brad's shoulders, "let's get you some food, huh? Frankie D.'s got some coffee coming and we can just—"

"Fuck off, junior." Brad shrugged Johnny away and turned back to Jax, his smarmy, drunken smile fixed in place. "I want to meet Gard's girlfriend. What's your name, honey?"

Gard pulled her closer, his fingers clamping harder on her upper arm, and she swore she could feel the furious pounding of his heart. She could feel how much energy it was taking for him to restrain himself.

"Jacqueline," she said, lifting her chin and staring back at Brad. She'd met more lecherous types in Hollywood than she could count. Big, bad Brad had nothing on them.

"Jacqueline," he said, his voice holding a hint of mockery. "Sounds . . . expensive."

"*Nique ta mere*," growled Gard under his breath, and it was so out of character, Jax swallowed a gasp. Even her brothers rarely used that particular, extremely vulgar, expression.

"Come on, Brad," cajoled Phil. "Time to eat something, buddy."

Meanwhile, Gard just stared at Brad, his eyes black with fury. Who was this? Who was—*Oh my God.* Suddenly it all clicked in Jax's head like an epiphany. *I found her with my partner. My first partner, Brad . . . In my apartment . . . In our bed.* Merde. *This* was Gard's first partner. The asshole who'd betrayed his trust and cheated with Gard's girlfriend.

Phil had put his arm around Brad's shoulders, and they started steering him away when Jax exclaimed in a cheerful, playful voice, "Wait! Wait a second! You're . . . *Brad*?"

"What are you doin'?" muttered Gard.

She winked at him, then looked at Brad, who'd turned around at the sound of his name. "Uh, yeah . . . ?"

"Oh my God, this is such a coincidence! I'm friends with—" She wracked her brain to remember the name of Gard's slut ex-girlfriend. "—Tiffany!"

"Huh," he said, a smug smirk moving back into place. "How d'ya know *her*?"

Ummm . . . "College. St. Joe's. Went there with this one too," she said, jabbing a thumb into Gard's stomach. "In fact, that's how we got together. I called his place looking for my old friend, Tiff, and he said she'd just moved out. We started gabbing, went out to dinner. The rest is history. Right, baby?" she asked, looking up at Gardener adoringly.

He gave her a dark look but inclined his head just slightly to play along. She winked at him again, then turned back to Brad.

"I did *eventually* track down Tiff, though. You know, to talk about old times . . . and she told me all about *you*! Brad! Brad, the police officer with a wife and two kids who used to be Gard's partner, right?"

"That's me," he said, leaning closer. His breath smelled of stale beer and her stomach rolled. "Ain't married anymore. If 'ole Tiff told you anything you'd like to try . . ."

Gard took a step forward. *Talk quick, Jax, or he's going to throw a punch!*

"Oh," she said, smiling at him with wide eyes. "I'm not really into that stuff."

She watched Brad's forehead crease in confusion. "Stuff?"

"I don't judge," said Jax holding up her palms. "If you need to wear adult diapers to, you know, get excited? Good for you."

A communal gasp was followed by a muffled snicker as Phil and Johnny exchanged shocked looks and started laughing.

"Wh-what? What're you—"

"And I'm just not into grown men calling me 'mommy.'" Jax cringed dramatically, then brightened. "She said she didn't mind spanking you . . . though she thought the way you'd say 'Wah, wah, wah' and pretend to cry was a little . . ." She shrugged. "I guess it's fun for some people, but I'm not a fan."

Brad's face had gone from pink to red to purple. "What the *fuck* are you—"

"When she said you liked crawling around on the floor and sucking your own thumb, I guess I just—"

With a chorus of snickers and hoots behind him, Brad lunged at her. "Shut up, you lying fucking cunt!"

She didn't know how everything happened so fast, but suddenly Brad was lying on the floor, knocked out cold, and Gard was rubbing his knuckles.

Phil, Johnny, and Saul stared down at Brad's body in various states of amusement and disbelief before looking up at Gard with wide eyes. Only Frankie D. had the presence of mind to say, "I guess the widdle baby needs a nap. Why don't you kids get out of here?"

Jax grinned at the older man, who winked at her with something that felt very much like admiration. She waved good-bye to Gard's friends as he took her other hand and pulled her to the exit.

As soon as their feet hit the sidewalk, Gard dropped her hand, bracing his palms on his knees as he let out a bellow of laughter that he'd been holding in ever since he'd realized what she was up to. Glory Lord, if he thought she was amazing before, she was downright miraculous now. When he stopped wheezing with laughter and could finally breathe again, he straightened, looking up at her.

"Duchess . . . you are . . ."

"Yes?" She was smiling at him, her shoulders shaking with laugher, her emeralds sparkling with mirth as she met his eyes.

"Magnificent."

She giggled with glee. "More like evil."

"No, no, no. He deserved it. But damn, woman," he said, grabbing her around the waist and pulling her up against his body. "How in the hell did you . . . ?"

"What? Come up with that?" She flattened her hands on his chest and shrugged. "I read about it in *Cosmo*."

He shook his head, utterly delighted with her. "His face! *Mon dieu*, it was priceless."

She sobered a little, her eyes and voice going soft. "He *did* deserve it. What he did to you was bad enough, but he was acting like such a jerk, provoking you by coming on to me!"

"He was always a bad drunk," said Gard darkly.

"I didn't want you to hit him and get in trouble."

"So much for good intentions. But I think Frankie'll cover for me. Brad was drunk enough; they'll just say he passed out."

"You've got a mean, fast punch, Gardener Thibodeaux."

He nodded. "Saw red when he got dirty with you. Sorry you had to hear that, *cher*."

"I have two brothers, remember?" She wrinkled her nose and shrugged it off. "Anyway, it was worth it."

He chuckled again. "He'll never live it down, you know. Never." He looked into her eyes, feeling wonder and tenderness, gratitude and excitement, well up inside of him like a wave. Leaning down, he pressed his lips to hers, pouring everything he felt into the feather touch before drawing back. "I like you, Jacqueline Rousseau. So much."

"I like you too."

Looking into her beautiful face, "like" felt so paltry, so stupid and small, for everything he was feeling for her. He wanted her to understand. He shook his head, leaning so close to her ear that he could feel the heat of her skin on his lips as he whispered, "I'm goin' to fall for you, Duchess. Hard. Don't know if it's just for now or forever, but if it's not okay with you, tell me now."

She shuddered in his arms, her breathing shaky as she murmured, "It's okay with me."

He sucked the lobe of her ear between his lips, teasing the soft pillow of skin before trailing his lips down the side of her neck and grinning as she tilted her head away from him to give him better access. Her skin smelled sweet and felt hot beneath his lips as he rested them for a moment over the racing pulse in her throat. Suddenly she whimpered, reaching frantically for his cheeks.

"Kiss me," she demanded, her deep-green eyes wide with lust and soft with pleasure as she looped her arms around his neck.

He was only too happy to comply.

Leaning forward, he seized her lips with his, lowering his hands to cup her ass as she arched her back, pushing her breasts into his chest. Her nipples beaded and he felt them, erect and hard against his chest, a reminder that she was just as aroused as he. And he was. Oh, *merde*, he was. His dick had started swelling the moment he'd pulled her into his arms, but as her tongue invaded his mouth, whatever blood was left in his head seemed to drain directly to his cock.

It had been such a long time since he'd had the privilege of kissing a woman the way he was kissing Jax, which not only engaged his body but—more and more—engaged his mind and heart as well. She was strong and beautiful, playful and sassy, the most fun he'd ever had, the hardest and fastest he'd ever fallen. And he fell . . . fell . . . fell deeper and deeper into the uncompromising attraction, tender longing, and fierce passion he felt for the woman in his arms.

She cupped his erection with the softness of her sex, cupped his head with her hands, her fingers buried in his hair, and leaned her forehead against his shoulder, her breasts pushing against his chest with every shallow breath.

"Come home with me tonight," he said, nuzzling her ear with his nose, grabbing the lobe between his teeth and flicking it with his tongue before letting it go. "Stay with me."

When she didn't answer, he leaned back to look into her eyes and found them worried, uncertain. She flinched just slightly, then tilted her head to the side, giving him a tentative little smile. "You should know that *want* and *should* are having an epic battle in my head right now."

"You just stole my line!" Chuckling softly, he kissed her forehead. "Who's winnin'?"

"I had fun tonight," she said, and her eyes, dark and warm, bore the truth of her words. "And I . . . I love what's happening between us. But . . ."

He swallowed. "Too soon?"

He could see it in her face—how much she wanted him to understand. How she wasn't turning him down or away so much as was trying not to rush things between them. He understood, of course, though, in his mind, her return to Hollywood loomed like a dark cloud, and he wanted to spend as much time with her as possible before she left him.

"Too soon," she confirmed.

He nodded, respecting the hell out of her for gently saying no when she wasn't quite ready to say yes. "Okay."

"But how about a lesson tomorrow?" she asked quickly, her eyes bright and hopeful. "My place? At three?"

"If you want."

"I *do* want," she said. "And . . . can you stay for a swim? And dinner? I'm a terrible cook, but I'm great at ordering."

"I tell you what," he said, "we'll have a lesson and a swim, and if you buy the Abita, I'll do the cooking."

"I heard you make a great gumbo," she said, clasping her hands together at the back of his neck.

He nodded, feeling happy even in the face of her gentle rejection. "We have a deal?"

"We have a deal," she said, leaning up on her toes and pulling his head down to hers to seal it with another scorching kiss.

Chapter 11

"The groin," he announced, giving her a dry look.

Standing across from him in the gym, she looked up at his serious face and tried desperately not to snicker.

Last night, she'd driven them back to Haverford, her fingers laced though his for the entirety of the ride as they talked about their families. She learned a little more about his father, who—from what she could gather—not only had been a very successful businessman but was Gard's best friend too. She sensed his deep sadness about losing his father, and though she shared a similar loss, she hadn't been as close to her own father and couldn't completely understand the depth of Gard's connection to his. However, she also told him all about Mad, Étienne, and J.C., with whom she did share a similar closeness. He gave her a sidelong look after she described her brothers and proclaimed them both "trouble," which made her chuckle because it was true.

After the intensity of their conversation outside of Club7, when they confessed their growing feelings for each other, there was something warm and reassuring about sharing details about their families. They were growing closer and deepening the bond between them.

When she woke up this morning, he'd been the first thought on her mind, the memory of their kisses making her sigh and the memory of his sweet words curling her toes. *I'm goin' to fall for you, Duchess. Hard. Don't know if it's just for now or forever, but if it's not okay with you, tell me now.* She loved that he hadn't pledged his undying love to her or something equally as silly. They hadn't known one another long enough for such declarations. The care he took in how he expressed his feelings made them feel ten times more real to her and mirrored her own perfectly. They were still from very different worlds. They were still getting to know each other. But they were also crashing into each other like they were fated to be together, and that they both felt it and recognized it was exhilarating.

Today he'd arrived a few minutes before three, and she'd kissed him hello, then taken his arm to guide him to the kitchen. She liked touching him, feeling the sinew of his muscles under her hand. But she also never wanted him to feel *blind* around her—worried about where to go or uncertain of bumping into something. When he was with her, she wanted him to tacitly rely on her eyes—she needed him to trust her, and it meant the world to her that he did.

When they reached the kitchen, she took the bags from him, emptying the contents onto the island counter.

"You'll, uh . . . you'll have to help me, Duchess," he'd said quietly. "I won't be able to see . . ."

"Can I be your sous chef?" she interrupted. "I'd love it!"

His face had instantly brightened, and she realized that the thought of needing her help (and telling her so) had weighed heavily on his heart.

"In fact," she said, placing raw sausage and chicken into the fridge, "since I can barely toast bread, I'm going to make it a point to memorize everything you teach me. I'll shock the pants off my sister and brothers when it's my night to host dinner and I actually *make* something instead of ordering!"

"I haven't made t'gumbo in ages, *cher*." He smiled at her. "But you won't be disappointed. My tantsy taught me well."

"Your . . . tantsy?"

"*Tante* means—"

"Aunt."

He nodded. "So tantsy is like . . . your mother's best friend or your father's first cousin. And in my case, my father's first cousin also looked after me and my sisters."

This surprised her a little. "Like a nanny?"

"Exactly."

"You had a nanny?"

He shrugged, looking away from her. "She was family."

She sensed that there was more to it than that and made a mental note to look up Gard's father on Google. He hadn't indicated that his childhood and upbringing had been exclusive or seeped in wealth, but he'd also gone to private school and had a nanny. He'd gone to a Northern school on full scholarship, but she'd noticed that his clothes were the same high quality as most of her peers. It would be gauche to ask about his socioeconomic status, but she couldn't deny that she was curious to learn more about him.

"Jax," he said in a stern voice, forcing her to return to the present. "The groin."

Standing across from him in the gym, she looked up at his serious face and tried desperately not to snicker. "I heard you the first time."

He rolled his eyes at her. "Are you ten years old?"

"Nope. Twenty-seven." She lowered her lashes, arched her back, and looked up at him, purring, "Can't you tell?"

"*Merde*, woman. Can we just get the lesson over with so we can make out?"

Her eyes widened, and her voice was a longing whisper. "*Oui.*"

He took a deep breath and exhaled. "The groin is, for obvious reasons, one of the most vulnerable parts of your assailant's body, which makes it a good target."

"As we learned last time," she supplied helpfully.

"Right. Thanks again for that." He took a deep, annoyed breath. "A knee to the nuts will make the toughest man fall."

"And did."

"Jax!" he exclaimed, looking exasperated. "It's hard enough—"

"Is it?"

"—to be alone with you, trying to teach you somethin', when all I want to do is . . ."

"Is . . . ?" she asked.

"Please, *cher*," he groaned.

"Please what?"

"Please let me teach you a couple of things."

"About . . . the groin?" she asked, unable to quit teasing him and knowing that he was just about at the end of his rope.

The thing was, she couldn't concentrate either. She'd kicked herself a million times since refusing him last night. Not that she'd made the wrong decision, because she wasn't ready to sleep with him quite yet . . . but his hands on her body? His lips blazing a trail of fire across her skin? *Yes, yes. Oh, please, yes.*

"Jax," he warned in a low, edgy voice. He stepped closer to her, his eyes black, his body all but stalking hers.

She let her eyes trail up his body provocatively, pausing at his pelvis and finally resting on his lips. "Yes?"

"*Ça va,*" he growled in surrender, his arm locking around her waist as he yanked her roughly up against his body. "You asked for it, Duchess."

His lips slammed into hers, their teeth clashing together as he lifted her into his arms and she locked her legs around his waist, reaching up to plow her fingers into his hair and pull his head down to hers. Taking three steps forward, he backed her up against the mirrored wall, his tongue plunging into her mouth to tangle with hers, and she welcomed him with a low moan of pleasure.

With his hands under her ass, he supported her body and tilted his head the other way, his tongue never leaving her mouth, twisting, sliding, gliding against hers in constant, frantic motion, fast and greedy, a preview of what it would be like to fuck her.

She broke away from his lips, taking a deep breath, and he hungrily trailed his lips down her throat, licking and sucking at will as she arched against him, her breasts pressing into his chest, frustrating both of them through the layers of her bra and his T-shirt. Drawing away, he looked her in the eyes and lowered his hands, helping her slide down the front of his body until she stood before him, the back of her head against the glass, her back bowed. Staring into her eyes, he reached behind her back, his fingers alighting on her bra clasp and separating each hook and eye until the two pieces of material flapped open at her sides.

Holding her eyes like a lifeline, he reached for her shoulders, found the straps of her bra, and slid them down her arms until the fabric fell to the floor between them with a soft *whoosh*. He trailed his fingers slowly, deliberately across the line of her collarbone until they met at the hollow of her neck. Then he dropped his eyes to look at her naked breasts.

Perfect orbs of olive-toned skin with dusky-tan areolas and pert almond-colored nipples heaved lightly with her rapid, shallow breathing, lifting to him as though in offering. He seized her eyes again and she lifted her chin, her lips parting as she met his fierce gaze.

"*Vous etes si belle que vous regarder est une souffrance,*" he said reverently, waiting for her lips to tilt up in acknowledgment before he leaned his head and licked a slow, gentle circle around her left nipple.

She arched her back, thrusting her chest forward, her nipple slipping between his lips, and he sucked greedily, then gently, flicking his tongue back and forth across the distended flesh until she gasped and whimpered. He kissed a small trail between her breasts, sucking her other nipple between his lips as his hands reached up to massage the first. Her skin was hot and soft, a little salty and a little sweet, and smelled of Jax—of lemons and rosemary, reminding him of bright smiles and too many questions, making his own body harder and hungrier, greedy to touch and taste more of her.

She reached for his cheeks, pulling his face up and kissing him, her fingers trailing down his neck to his back until she reached the hem of his shirt. She pushed it up, her palms sliding flat against his skin and making him shiver. Breaking off their kiss, he reached behind his neck and pulled the shirt over his head, then pulled her against him, the hard, damp points of her nipples pressing into the naked skin of his chest and making him groan with longing.

"Lie down with me," he growled softly, bending down to sit on a cushioned mat and pulling her with him. Grinning down at him, she straddled his lap, letting her breasts rake against his chest until she was fully seated, his fully erect cock sandwiched between them. He wrapped his arms around her and leaned her back until she was lying beneath him, and he moved experimentally on top of her, his erection sliding along the seam of her workout pants and making her gasp.

He kissed her again—kissed her chin, her throat, and the hollow at the base of her neck. Still lower, he took her pebbled nipple into his mouth as his hand slid lower, over the soft skin of her belly, pausing at the waistband of her pants for just a moment before slipping into her panties.

She arched up, whimpering as he razed her breast with his teeth and his fingers slid into the slick folds of her sex, finding the nub of her clit swollen and hot. He slid his lips to her other nipple, sucking it between his lips as his middle finger began a slow, circular motion over her sensitive flesh. Her breathing quickened and small noises of arousal lifted from her throat, making him harden like rock, throbbing behind the material of his sweat pants as Jax buried the back of her head into the mat, gasping and moaning her pleasure.

He increased the motion of his finger as he leaned up to kiss her lips. His tongue slid against hers and she reached frantically for his head, arching her back as he continued to caress her clit. His cock throbbed for release, and he thrust forward against her hip as her whimpers grew louder and deeper. He pushed against her again and again, still rubbing her slick, satiny skin until he felt her muscles tighten to a breaking point, making her cry out as they released in contractions beneath his finger.

He watched her face—her beautiful face—as she climaxed, and when she opened her eyes, as dark as pine trees at midnight, he felt his own release imminent. As she rode out the last shudders of her pleasure, he removed his hand from her pants and slid the same damp fingers around his cock, gliding his fingers up and down his erection with the slickness of her juices and quickly spending himself in hot, rhythmic spurts.

He fell back on the mat, his body slack with satisfaction beside hers. He could hear the sound of his own breathing in his ears, deep yet uneven, a little jagged, a little fast. Turning to the side, he faced her.

She stared up at the ceiling, quiet and still but for a tear that slipped from the corner of her eye and trickled into her hair.

"Jax?" he said.

She turned her head to look at him, her eyes deep and green, swimming with tears.

Gard leaned up on one elbow, reaching with his free hand to cup her cheek. "Duchess. What is it?"

She clenched her jaw, looking away from him, back up at the ceiling. More tears slipped from her eyes, but she let them fall, and Gard didn't whisk them away. Was it too fast? Too much for her?

"Did I hurt you?" he asked.

She shook her head, closing her eyes for a second as if she was in pain.

"Then . . . ?"

She sobbed softly, opening her eyes and turning her head again to look at him. "It was beautiful."

Relief coursed through him like a drug, and he took a deep breath, filling his diaphragm and then exhaling slowly. Leaning down, he touched his lips to hers, gently, tenderly. When he drew away, she reached up to cover his hand with hers.

"Do you always cry at beautiful things, *cher*?" he asked, smiling into her eyes.

"Not always." She chuckled and sniffled at the same time. "Sometimes."

"There's no shame in it," he said, rolling her gently to her side and pulling her half-naked body against his chest. His forearm rested beneath the weight of her naked breasts, and his chest pushed into her back, his damp pants flush against her Lycra-covered backside.

"Was it . . . for you?" she asked softly.

"Beautiful?" He answered his own question without hesitation: "*Oui.*"

"Have you . . . I mean, have you been with a lot of women, Gard?"

He leaned forward and kissed the back of her neck. "That I cared about? No, *cher.* Not many. You?"

"I've never been with a woman," she said, with just a hint of sass in her voice. Then she added, "No. I haven't been with a lot of men."

"How'd you keep them all away?"

She turned in his arms, lying on her back, looking up into his eyes. "I said no."

He brushed his thumb over her nipple, and she gasped softly.

"Why'd you say yes to me?"

Her eyes were soft and tender as they searched his. "Because this feels right."

"Yes, Duchess," he said, leaning down to brush her lips with his, "it does."

Her smile was blinding as she reached up to swipe any remaining tears away. Then suddenly she sat up, reaching for her bra and slipping her arms through the straps. "I'm dying for a swim. You?"

I'm dying to lie here until we start round two, he thought, but he grinned at her instead. "I guess I could use one." He sat up, leaning back on his hands, watching her as she adjusted her breasts into the cups of the bra and fastened it in the back. "I miss having a pool."

"Did you have one in your apartment building? In Philly?"

"No. At home. When I was a kid."

She nodded, her eyes narrowing just slightly as she stood up and put her hands on her hips. "Private schools, nannies, and swimming pools. What kind of gardener was your dad anyway?"

"A good one," he said, jumping up beside her and gesturing to the door. "Lead the way."

She gave him a look that said she wanted to ask more, but instead she turned and headed through the door that led to the hallway. He grabbed his duffel bag from the floor and followed, his thoughts turning organically to his parents.

When his parents met, his mother was a runner-up at the 1979 Miss New Orleans pageant, and his father had just secured a deal that would change his fledgling business, Thibodeaux Gardening Service, into a company that would eventually become the largest and most high-end landscape design company in southeastern Louisiana, Thibodeaux Landscapers, LLC. So yes, he and his sisters had grown up in a mansion and attended private school . . . but that didn't change the fact that his father had grown up on a small Cajun farm located on the banks of the Bayou Teche in Breaux Bridge, the heart of Cajun country. Didn't change the fact that his father's strong country accent would always be a barrier between him and the New Orleans elite. Didn't change the fact that some of the old-money kids at his school had whispered "swamp Cajun" under their breath whenever he was within earshot, even though Gard's mother's pedigree was better than some of theirs.

It was an early lesson that money couldn't buy you everything. It made life nicer and more comfortable, but it didn't change the fact that his father was a Thibodeaux from the bayou, even if his mother's maiden name was Heard. It couldn't buy you acceptance, and it certainly couldn't buy you happiness—it was up to you to find, make, or pursue it yourself.

Jax slid open the sliding glass door to the pool deck, and he followed her outside into the soupy late-afternoon heat.

"You'd think," he said, "that growin' up in Louisiana would've given me a high tolerance for humidity."

She stopped at a lounge chair and turned to face him. "No?"

He shook his head. "No. I hate it as much as I ever did. But it's not half as bad up here."

He watched, his expression ravenous, as she shimmied out of the black Lycra workout pants she'd been wearing, revealing black-and-blue boy shorts that matched her sports bra. She was all tan skin and long legs. Tan skin that still tasted sweet and salty on his tongue . . . long legs that had been wrapped around his waist fifteen minutes ago.

"Damnnnnn, Jax."

She grinned. "Yeah?"

He shook his head and sighed. "Where can I change?"

"Wherever you want," she said, running over to the pool and jumping in.

Well, *merde*. He didn't know where a dressing room was, and she knew it. Left with little alternative, he turned around and, before he could think better of it, pulled down his pants, offering her a fine view of his ass as he leaned down to unzip his duffel bag and pull out some swim trunks. From behind him, he heard her hoot with appreciative laughter, which made him chuckle softly. Looking over his shoulder, all he could see was some blurry gray slate and a large blob of aqua, but he asked into the void, "Like the view?"

"Can't think of a better one!" came her voice.

He pulled up his swimsuit, then turned around. "Show's over."

"That's sad," she said.

"If you're lucky, there might be an encore later."

He heard her clap and giggle.

"Jax?" he asked.

"Huh?"

His insecurities kicked in. He could either ask her what was between them . . . or take the chance of bumping into something and tripping while making his way to her . . . or—

"There's nothing between you and me," she said. "Run for it!"

And that's when it happened.

That was the moment.

His heart burst with love for her, and he ran across the hot slate and jumped.

Three hours later, they sat across from each other at a table on the pool deck, a steamy pot of gumbo between them, their bowls licked clean.

"That was soooo good," said Jax, holding a glass of wine in her hands and finding his bare feet under the table.

He'd sat on the kitchen counter instructing her on how to make his tantsy's gumbo while she did the work, occasionally stopping to give him a kiss or brush up against him. She browned the chicken and sausage in butter and oil, then put them in a stew pot. For the first time ever, she made a roux from the drippings mixed with flour. Under his supervision, she chopped the onions, garlic, peppers, celery, tomatoes, and okra, then placed it all in the pot with a splash of Worcester sauce.

"That's it?" she'd asked, feeling delighted as she set the timer for two hours. "That's easy!"

They'd headed back outside to the pool, where they'd laid down side by side on lounge chairs, holding hands and saying little as they baked in the sun, then cooled off again in the pool. He'd grabbed her and held her, kissing her wet lips, his fingers threaded through her soaked hair. And Jax had wrapped her legs around his body, feeling the hardness of his erection through his bathing suit as they kissed, loving this time together.

Loving.

Loving.

The word had flitted so effortlessly into her head, but it had also made her pause.

Is that what this was? The beginning of love? Is this how it started? Two people who'd grown up in two different parts of the world, crashed into each other on a dark night, and somehow recognized some potential—some fragile, magical possibility in each other's eyes, in one another's company. *Love.* Was she falling in love with Gardener Thibodeaux? Because in twenty-seven years, she'd never felt this way before, and it was frightening and exhilarating, and the thought of ruining it or losing it was a constant and growing ache.

"So you liked t'gumbo?" he asked, grinning at her as he took another sip of the decadent 2012 Montepulciano that she'd discovered in the small wine cellar located in the basement of Le Chateau.

She nodded. "It was delicious."

"Next time I'll bring French bread to sop it up."

"Sopping" one's food wasn't something that Jax had grown up doing, but she couldn't wait to try it. "Deal."

"Can I ask you somethin'?"

"Sure," she said, picking up her glass and taking a sip.

"How long you plannin' to stay here? I mean, I assume you're headed back to Hollywood at some point, but . . ."

Jax took a deep breath, unprepared for the way the question stung. She had decided to stay in Philly, and suddenly it felt weird to share that. She didn't want to think of their relationship as temporary, and it hurt her a little that he did. "I'm not sure what my plans are."

He'd been sitting back in his chair, but now he leaned forward. "Just so we're clear . . . no matter how long you're here, I want to spend as much time with you as I can."

"Oh." Her clenched heart relaxed, and tears of relief pricked her eyes. "I want that too."

"You still have a place out there?"

She shook her head. "No." Pausing, she looked behind her, at the yellow stone of Le Chateau, feeling miserable even *talking* about leaving. "Lately, I've been thinking . . ."

"What?"

Could she trust him with her wishes? With her longings and hopes?

"Well, I've been thinking about buying *this* place."

"*Buyin'* it? Doesn't your family already *own* it?"

"Not exactly. My *mother* owns it. And she doesn't like it. And despite her . . . *funds*, she lives a very expensive life in Paris. Selling Le Chateau would support her spending habits."

He cocked his head to the side, his eyes holding hers intently. "You're afraid she'll sell it?"

She took a gulp of wine, swallowing it over the sudden lump in her throat, and nodded. "Yes."

"Duchess, it's a big house—"

"—for one small girl. I know. My sister said that too."

She watched as he squinted, looking around the pool area. Not that he could see the details of the landscaping, but she knew it would be expensive to maintain. Not to mention the house itself was a massive mansion, enough for a family of six or eight, and the taxes, *merde*—His eyes focused back on hers.

"It's a big decision."

"I see your mind spinning," she said softly. "It's a ridiculous thought."

"It's not ridiculous," he said quickly. "But it's an awful lot to take on."

"I'd have to hire someone," she said, "to look after it for me, I guess."

"A *team* of someones," said Gard. "House, grounds, pool, pool house . . ."

Her heart clutched as she placed her wine glass back on the table. "Let's not talk about it anymore."

"Jax," he said gently, and when she looked up at him, his face was blurry from the tears in her eyes. "Anythin's possible if you want it bad enough."

She swallowed, forcing a grin as she nodded. "Sure."

"If you have the money, you can—"

"How about one more swim?" she asked, standing up and unwrapping the towel around her waist. She brushed at her eyes as she ran over to the pool and jumped in, the cool water like heaven on her hot face.

He was right. She hadn't really thought it through. It wasn't just about the money—she had the money . . . it was about the care and maintenance of an estate, hiring staff and paying taxes and insurance. In addition, she still hadn't figured out if it was possible to shoot *Philadelphia Vice* on location. If not, then what? She loved being a producer, and she wanted to produce another project. Would she *need* to return to LA to make that happen? Too many questions to sort through and no immediate answers made her feel helpless.

She heard a splash behind her, and suddenly Gard was holding her, pinning her arms to her sides as he pulled her back against his chest. His lips were close to her ear when he said, "Duchess. Don't be sad. You'll figure it out. If you want, I'll help you figure it out."

She leaned her head back against his shoulder, closing her eyes. "I never thought I'd get to twenty-seven and be so clueless about what happens next in my life. I hate feeling helpless."

"You're not, though," he said gently. "You're smart and capable, rich as Midas. I can see you gettin' stronger and stronger every day, *cher*. Just decide what you want and make it happen."

What if I want Le Chateau? What if I want to produce Philadelphia Vice *here? So I can still see my siblings every Thursday? And be best friends with Daisy and Skye? What if each thing I want is a puzzle piece, but they belong to different puzzles, and I can't figure out how to fit them all together? What if I lose the best things chasing after the wrong things? What if I just want to be with you?*

She wrestled her arms free and turned in his arms to face him, giving him the abridged version. "What if I want my house and my show and . . . you?"

"Duchess," he whispered, his eyes soft, a grin tipping his lips up. "Those things aren't mutually exclusive."

"Are you sure?" she asked, searching his eyes for reassurance.

"I'm sure," he whispered, leaning forward to touch his lips to hers in a gentle, loving kiss.

"Jaxy! Hey, Jaxy! Who's the new man?"

Her body went rigid in Gard's arms as she looked in the direction of the voice, which came from the edge of the pool house.

Click. Flash. Click click click. Flash.

She blinked her eyes, blinded by the camera's flash.

"Holy hotness! Jaxy Rousseau making out in the family pool!" said the intruder, his voice slimy and excited.

"Gard!" she gasped, whipping her eyes to his. "Help!"

He released her immediately, swimming the length of the pool in a moment, then leaping out and racing toward the sound of the photographer's voice.

"Who are you? Who the *hell* are you?" he roared, but in his haste, he tripped over a pool chair and landed flat on his face on the pool deck.

"Ooo-hooo!" exclaimed the photographer with delight. "Picked a real winner with this one, Jaxy!"

"Get out!" she screamed, scrambling to the side of the pool. "I'm calling the police. I'll have you arrested for trespassing!"

"No need to tell me twice," he said. "You take care now!"

She pulled her body from the pool, racing to Gard, who lay motionless on the slate deck, blood streaming from his head.

"Gard? Gard?" She knelt beside him, sobbing, feeling more lost and more alone than ever.

Her fortress had been breached.

Her heart sank with despair.

Chapter 12

Pounding.

And fuzzy.

Those were the first two things that occurred to him when he slowly opened his eyes, wincing at the bright light before trying to focus. He blinked several times, trying to sit up, then groaned as the pounding in his head increased. Easier to let his head fall back onto the pillow.

"Gard? Gard, can you hear me?"

Jax.

He gasped, his fingers twisting into the fabric at his sides.

She's in trouble. She needs me.

"Can you get the doctor? I think he's waking up," she said. Then softly, close to his ear, "Gard? *Tu m'entends? Mon coeur, c'est moi. Jax. La duchesse.*"

He knew exactly who she was. And whatever else she said didn't matter. She'd just called him her "heart" in her perfect, pristine Parisian French, and it was by far the sweetest thing he'd ever heard in all his life.

He opened his eyes again, focusing on her face, which was hovering close to his.

"*Mon coeur?*" he asked.

"Gard," she whispered.

"*Mon coeur?*" he asked again, searching her eyes, needing to be sure she'd said it, needing to know if she meant it.

"*Oui.*" Tears rolled down her cheeks as she nodded her head. "*Mon coeur.*"

"Don't cry, Duchess," he rasped, closing his eyes again, his hand sliding over the bed sheets in her general direction, stopping when she clasped it, threading her fingers between his and raising his hand to her lips. She pressed her lips lovingly to his skin, then rubbed her cheek against the back of his hand.

"I was scared."

"I'm . . . I'm sorry," he mumbled, trying to remember what had happened, what had scared her.

"I was scared for you."

He cracked his eyes open and sighed. "I'm sorry I scared you." He paused. "Why did I—I can't remember . . . ?"

And then, suddenly, he did.

He winced, groaning as the memories came rushing back. He'd been running in the general direction of the photographer's voice only to bang his knees on something hard and—and, *oh, merde!*—face plant on her pool deck. Christ, he'd been useless to her. Less than useless. An embarrassment to her and himself.

"Fuuuuck," he muttered.

"Watch your mouth," she said gently, squeezing his fingers and giving him a little smile. "There's a lady here."

"Jax," he groaned, wishing he could crawl into a hole and hide. Not only had he let her down; he'd left her totally unprotected while some piece-of-shit paparazzo trash was hunting her. He winced, closing his eyes. Glory Lord, he could die of shame.

"No!" she said, her tone fierce. Her fingers abandoned his to reach up and clutch his chin. She forced him to face her. "Don't you *dare* do that!"

"Do what, *cher*?" he asked, opening his eyes but keeping them averted as best he could. He couldn't bear to look at her after failing her so completely.

"Look away from me. Be embarrassed. You were trying to protect me."

Her words only served to make him feel more ashamed. It was the bottom of the bell jar, the lowest low. He'd acted on instincts from an old life of serving and protecting, only to discover—to finally, finally be forced to accept—that that life was long gone. And he was joke for trying to hold onto it.

"Did quite a job of it too," he said softly, still unwilling to look at her.

"Gard," she said, her voice breaking. She took a deep breath, and when she exhaled, it was jagged and soft. "You don't understand."

He glanced at her. "Understand what?"

"Seeing you . . . lying there . . . with blood coming out of your—" She touched her own forehead lightly and took another shaking breath. "It put everything in perspective. I've been . . . feeling sorry for myself. Hiding. More scared than angry. But in that moment? With you lying there bleeding? I thought, *The rest be damned!* I got angry. I finally. Got. *Furious.*"

He stared at her, waiting for her to continue.

"*No one* has a right to hunt me like that, to trespass on private property, to intimidate me, to make me feel unsafe, to invade my personal space. No one. And I *won't* stand for it." Her voice grew stronger as she spoke, her posture straighter and stronger. "I've already spoken to a lawyer. I'm pressing charges. Le Chateau is private property, so if those pictures show up anywhere, I'll sue whoever took them and whoever buys and prints them."

He nodded, wincing from a fresh stab of pain. "Good for you, Jax."

She took a deep breath and sighed, cocking her head to the side.

"You got eleven stitches," she said, her voice wavering again as she reached for his hand. "Oh, Gard. I'm so sorry."

"Don't be sorry, Duchess," he said, looking at her red-rimmed eyes and feeling them like a punch to the gut.

"If something had happened to you . . ."

"I'll be okay."

"I already told the hospital that you'd be coming home with me. I'll take care of you until you feel—"

"No, *cher*," he said gently, squeezing her hand before untangling their fingers. "No."

"Gard . . ." she started, an edge in her wobbly voice.

It was bad enough that he'd wiped out so spectacularly, failing to protect her. But to be downgraded from potential lover to feeble patient? No. He couldn't bear it. Better to break things off now.

"I think maybe our journey together ends here, Duchess."

"No," she said, shaking her head back and forth as she clasped her hands together beside him on the white sheets. "No, it doesn't."

"You told me once that you came back to Philly because you wanted someone to anchor you, to protect you, to make you feel safe."

"*You* do those things for me," she said. "I've felt more anchored, more protected, and more safe since the moment I ran into you that nigh—"

"How can you say that?" he demanded angrily, raising his voice, feeling his face twist into a sneer. "I'm a blind man! How can I be an anchor for you? How can I protect you or keep you safe, woman? You saw what happened when I tried!"

"We're not *cave people*!" she yelled back. "I don't need a Neanderthal goon to follow me around with a club beating photographers away! What I need is—"

"Some sightless joke of a—"

He supposed she did what she did next because she couldn't bear to hit his injured face, so she went for the next most vulnerable spot . . . per his instruction. She slapped him as hard as she could in the nuts.

"Ahhhhk! Arrrr. Gah!" he groaned, reaching down under the sheet to cover his penis before looking up at her in horror. "*Merde! Pourquoi?*"

Shit! Why?

Her eyes were narrowed to slits of green, and her voice was low and lethal. "Don't you *ever* call yourself a joke again. Not to me. Not ever. Do you understand?"

If he'd thought her fierce before, when she'd grabbed his chin, she was downright scary now. Thank God the blankets over his body had absorbed some the shock of her smack, but his balls still ached.

He frowned at her, growling between clenched teeth, "*Oui.*"

"I'm sorry I hit you," she said softly, glancing at his groin with guilty eyes.

He grumbled, "Kinda gettin' used to it, Duchess."

"Can I please finish what I was saying?"

He nodded.

"I don't need you to be my personal policeman. I can protect myself. You're teaching me how, remember? Don't you see? Before I ran into you that night, I had no idea what I was doing with my life, what came next. No plan. Just a frightened girl hiding away in her childhood home. Now? I've found a script I love. I'm trying to figure out how to produce it. I have a meeting later this week, did I tell you that?"

He shook his head, his heart swelling with love for her as she told him the ways that his presence in her life had already improved it for the better.

"As for feeling safe?" She took his hand and pressed it to her lips again. "You *do* make me feel safe. You take the loneliness away. You make me feel beautiful. And grounded. And maybe that's because you're a gardener . . ." She sniffled, laughing weakly at her own bad joke. ". . . but I think it's because I'm falling in love with you." She gulped, dropping his eyes and clasping his hand in hers.

After a long second—the exact amount of time it took for him to process her beautiful words, to fully understand and accept their meaning and let them settle into his heart—he took a deep breath and said, "What's the first rule?"

She raised her chin and her eyes found his. "Don't ever look away."

"That's right," he said, searching her face and knowing that if he didn't turn her away right now, right here, he was choosing her, choosing to give them a chance. He nodded, unable to keep his lips from wobbling into a small, grateful smile. "Now kiss me, *cher*."

Tears brightened her eyes as she stared at him for just a moment before giggling softly with a look of surprise and relief and then leaned forward as he had asked, pressing her lips to his.

Two days later, after a concussion had been ruled out and Gard had seen a surgical ophthalmologist to ensure his eyes hadn't suffered further as a result of his fall, he was permitted to leave the hospital with Jax, who pulled up in her mother's Mercedes and grinned at him as a nurse wheeled him out to the curb.

Standing up with a growl of annoyance as soon as the chair stopped moving, he practically leapt into the car. "Please get me out of here."

"With pleasure!" she said, stepping on the gas with glee. She turned to him once they pulled out of the parking lot. "How are you feeling?"

"My head still hurts a little."

"The doctor said your eyes are okay."

"Thank God." He turned to her. "Not like I can afford to lose what I have."

"Well, luckily you didn't." She grinned at him. "Let's get you back to my place and I'll—"

"Jax," he said, his voice serious, "I don't need to stay with you. I don't need a nurse. I'm fine."

She didn't turn to look at him, but her face fell, all the joy that she'd felt anticipating his more-constant presence in her life fading like a dream in the morning. Honestly, the hospital's recommendation that he stay with "a friend" for a week had just been a convenient excuse for her to ask him. She wanted him in her space. She wanted him around all the time. And the idea that he would simply go back to the Englishes' gardener's cottage, which felt ridiculously far away, fell like lead on her heart.

"But I was—I mean, I wanted to take care of you," she said softly, feeling bereft at the idea that she was going to be deprived of the opportunity.

"Well, fair enough," he answered evenly, "but only if you let me take care of you too."

She took a deep breath, stopping at a stoplight, her joy returning as quickly as it had fled. He wasn't saying no. She held her smile back, turning to face him.

He gave her a no-nonsense look. "You have to let me upgrade your security system, okay? I have some friends who can come and take a look. I want to be sure you're—"

"Done!" she said, leaning over the bolster to kiss him quickly. "Yes. Thank you."

"That's not all." He smiled back at her, shaking his head. "I still have to help out Felix too."

"Of course," she said, nodding at him with what she hoped were wide, compliant eyes.

"And I can help you with that script if you need me to," he offered.

"That would be great."

His eyes darkened. Just a touch. But enough for her to notice.

"And I still owe you a lesson."

"Oh. Right. The . . . groin," she said, her cheeks flushing with heat as she recalled the last time they'd started that lesson.

"And Duchess?" he said, his voice low and seductive as he leaned over the bolster and pressed his lips to her bare shoulder. "One more thing."

"Hmm?" she moaned, closing her eyes for just a moment until the car behind her beeped. Her eyes flew open and she pressed on the gas.

"Just to be clear . . . if I'm stayin' at your place, I'm not stayin' in some guest room. If I'm sleepin' at your place, I'm sleepin' next to you."

Her breath caught, and suddenly it didn't feel like there was enough room in the car for both of them. "I . . ."

She knew, beyond any shadow of a doubt, that he wasn't talking about sex. Jax knew that he cared for her, and she knew that he would respect her wishes and timeline when it came to intimacy. But her own words returned to her like a boomerang, whispering sweetly in her head, *I'm falling in love with you*, and without a hint of uncertainty, she knew that she didn't need to wait anymore and that everything he wanted was exactly what she wanted too.

"I guess . . . I guess friends do that sometimes," she said, sighing as she cast him a quick glance.

He reached for the hand closest to him, pulling it gently from the steering wheel and pressing his lips to her skin. "*Oui, Duchesse.* I guess they do."

They stopped by Haverford Park to give Gard a chance to speak to Felix for a few minutes and grab some of his belongings. He explained what had happened at Jax's house over the weekend, how he'd been injured and how he wanted to make sure her place was secure. Felix had nodded in understanding, telling Gard to take the rest of the week off to see to his head and to Jax, for which Gard was grateful. He'd packed a bag with some extra clothes and toiletries, then gotten back into her waiting car.

He wasn't sure what had come over him when he told her that he wouldn't come stay at Le Chateau unless he was sleeping in her bed, and truly he didn't expect to suddenly have sex with her tonight (though he couldn't deny he was hopeful). It embarrassed him that he'd injured himself in pursuit of her safety, but she didn't seem to think less of him for it. Well, if she could live with it, he could too. But under no circumstances would he allow the passion they shared to be tempered by his "condition." Either she saw him as a man she desired as much as he desired her or he'd just as soon leave Pennsylvania and never return.

Now, however, he'd lobbed a curveball into their relationship, and he wasn't positive what she'd do with it. She seemed awfully skittery as she pulled into the driveway.

Cutting the engine, she turned to him. "Do you want to, um, settle in?"

Holding her eyes, he nodded. "Yep."

"In—" She cleared her throat. "—my room?"

"Yep."

"Do you want me to come?"

The breath in his lungs froze and held. And he was pretty sure time just fucking stopped. He stared at her for a moment, his eyes wide.

"Ohhh." She whimpered like she was in pain, her eyes flying open as she realized what she'd said. "I mean, c-come *with* you? To my room? Or do you want some privacy?"

"I want you to come, Duchess," he said, exhaling with a huge grin as two deep spots of color pinkened her cheeks.

"I didn't mean . . . Oh God. I really didn't mean—"

He pulled his duffel from the backseat. "Why don't you show me where to put my bag?"

"Yes! Your bag. Show you. Yes," she said, practically bolting from the car.

He opened his door, swinging his body out of the car and swallowing a chuckle as he followed her to the front door. He pushed it shut behind him with his foot and just about had to run across the foyer to catch up with her. It was like she was on autopilot, all but running up the grand staircase and not daring to look back around at him. Wow. She was nervous. Really nervous.

He checked out her ass in a short butter-yellow skirt as he walked up the steps just behind her. It was curvy and round, and he was dying to feel its naked softness beneath his fingers. However, in light of her jitters, sharing such a thought probably wouldn't help right now. In fact . . .

"Jax?"

"Hmmm?"

"I'm not going to jump on you, *cher*."

"Oh," she said with a slightly crazy-sounding, high-pitched little laugh. "I know." But she still didn't glance back at him.

When they reached the second floor, he stopped following her, crossing his arms over his chest and trying to get his bearings. The staircase went up through the center of the house, which meant that there were long galleries off to the left and right. He couldn't make out much detail, of course. The red carpeting extended in both directions, which was helpful for finding his way back to the stairs. Looked like the walls were cream-colored. No. Cream and gold. Wallpaper? He squinted. Maybe. Sort of looked like there was a pattern beneath the color, but he'd have to get closer to be sure. He looked up to see a brass chandelier over his head and what appeared to be two more in the wings to his left and right, brightening the ceiling at intervals. He numbered them one through five in his head. Once he knew the doors located under those chandeliers, he'd be able to find his way easier. Sitting room at chandelier one. Bathroom at two. Stairs at three. Jax's room at four . . . et cetera, et cetera. A map in his head based on colors, lights, and numbers. He'd have to remind her not to turn off the lights at night too, or else he could easily lose his way.

He sighed, taking in his new surroundings as best he could, waiting for her to realize that he wasn't following her anymore. Before he took another step, they needed to talk.

"Gard?" she asked from a distance to his left. He turned to the sound of her voice but couldn't make her out well until she turned around and started walking back to him. Finally she came into focus. "You coming?"

"Let me ask you somethin'," he said, looking into her bright-green emeralds. "Where do *you* want me to sleep?"

She blinked at him. "You said you're sleeping with me."

"That's not what I asked you, *cher*. Where do *you* want me to sleep?" He uncrossed his arms, taking a step toward her. "Because, to tell you the truth, you seem pretty nervous, and I don't want that. I want you to be comfortable. So you tell me, Duchess. You want me to stay in a guest room? I will. You want me to stay downstairs on the couch? I will. I'm here, Jax. I'm here and I'm not goin' anywhere till you tell me we're done, *mon coeur*, so you call it. Where do you want me?"

She flinched, looking so beautiful and young and vulnerable, it made his heart throb with tenderness for her.

"*Mon coeur*?" she murmured.

He took another step toward her, placing his palm over his heart, meeting her gaze with surrender and hope. "It's yours for the takin', Jax."

"With me," she said softly, but with a certainty she'd been missing a minute before. She held out her hand to him. "I want you to sleep with me."

He placed his hand in hers, letting her pull him along. She walked halfway down the corridor, stopped between chandeliers one and two, then stepped through an open door into a room. Reaching back, he closed the door behind them.

When he turned to face her, she was standing beside the bed, stepping out of her heeled sandals. Stepping forward, she pulled his bag from his shoulder, setting it down on the floor.

When she lifted her eyes to his, they were so full of aching tenderness, his breath caught, his heart clenched, and his chest tightened with the certainty that this woman was his one in a million, that she—and *only* she—held the key to his happiness in her hands.

"You're so beautiful, it hurts to look at you," he said, the words coming from a pure, visceral place of longing, of certainty, of gratitude, and yes, of love. "What do you want, *mon coeur*?"

"I want you to make love to me," she whispered.

He placed his hands on her face, staring deeply into her soft, darkened eyes, then lowered his lips to hers.

Jax had known, after seeing him facedown on the pool deck with dark-red blood seeping from his head, that her feelings for him were deep and intense and real. It no longer mattered that they'd met by chance, that he was an ex-cop gardener and she a movie producer heiress, that his accent was Cajun and hers Parisian, that they'd fallen for each other so quickly and without restraint. None of it mattered. Her heart had already ruled on the matter—every other consideration be damned. She wanted him in her life. And having him here, in her home, in her bedroom, with their feelings for one another propelling them both forward, made this the only place on earth she wanted to be.

She'd worn a cream-colored linen tank top and short, tailored yellow linen skirt to pick him up at the hospital, and now she felt his fingers on the zipper of her skirt, pulling it down as he kissed her. She wiggled her hips just a little, and the light fabric slipped down her legs, pooling around her bare feet and leaving her in cream-colored satin panties and her tank top. As he dragged his lips to her throat, his fingers trailed over the material of the top, finding the three little pearl buttons at the back of her neck and slowly unfastening them. Then he stepped back and drew the tank over her head, dropping it to the floor, holding her gaze all the while. He reached up, pulling a pearl comb from her chignon, which released her waves of onyx hair, and he threaded his fingers through it from her temples to her shoulder blades. As his fingers found the clasp of her bra, she held her breath, then released it as the lingerie slipped down her arms, joining her skirt and top on the floor.

Standing before him in nothing but panties, she felt her cheeks flush with heat.

"You are so beautiful, Jax. My beautiful duchess," he said softly, as though mesmerized, his fingers touching down gently beneath her ears, following the curve of her neck to her shoulders, trailing down her arms then clasping her hips, his palms just covering the waistband of her underwear.

Still staring up at her, he dropped fluidly to his knees, and she gasped to see the contrast of his thick, wavy hair just in front of her still-covered sex. Her blood coursed through her veins like liquid lightning, making her hot all over, making her long for more—more words, more touching, more everything.

"I want to taste you, *cher*," he said, his fingers smoothing gently from her hips to the waistband of her panties. He tugged them a little, and they slipped over the curve of her ass, gliding down her legs with a whisper and leaving her completely naked to him.

For the first time, he dropped her eyes, his gaze searing a path down her body, pausing at her lips, her throat, her breasts, her stomach, and ending at the small thatch of soft black curls covering her sex.

So exposed, with the bright light of early evening streaming into her room, she knew she should have felt at least a small flare of modesty, but she didn't. She felt electric. She felt powerful. She felt trust. And more than anything, she felt a lust so consuming, so hot and demanding, she had to draw her fingers into a fist to keep them from plunging into his hair to shove his face forward.

"Lie down," he said without looking up, his palms hot on the skin of her hips.

She stepped back until her thighs hit the side of her bed, then sat down, lowering herself until her back was flat on the bedspread but her feet were flat on the floor. When she placed her hands on the bed and started to push back, he stopped her, flattening his hand over her damp mound.

"No, *cher*," he said, reaching for her legs and looping them over his shoulders, spreading her wide. "Like this."

"Gard," she whimpered, closing her eyes, her body as tight as a wire, her insides coiled in anticipation. She curled her fingers into the soft fabric by her sides, trying to catch her breath as she felt his thumbs spread the lips of her sex.

She threw an arm over her eyes as she felt his breath kiss the sensitive folds of skin, and she cried out when the heat of his tongue circled her aching clit.

"Oh, *merde*," he groaned, his tongue lapping her throbbing flesh in one long stroke from base to hood, and making her shiver, "you taste perfect. Sweet. Hot."

She tried to catch her breath, swallowing as she pressed closer to his face, trying to concentrate on the pressure of his hands clutching her thighs to slow down the fast build to orgasm. He swiped his tongue around her slit again, then gently sucked the pulsing bud between his lips before releasing. She cried out an "unh" sound, moving her hips as her breathing became more and more shallow.

"Did you go to school for this?" she half-moaned, half-whimpered.

"No." He chuckled softly, a low, rich sound that vibrated against her sensitive skin, and she clenched her teeth, burying her head back into the mattress. "But remember, Duchess, you asked if I wanted you to come, and it's all I've thought about since. The answer is *yes*."

He took her clit between his lips again, but this time he suckled harder, two fingers entering the slick opening of her body and hooking forward to press on the throbbing wall of her sex. Jax's hips bucked off the bed as she exploded into a million tiny pieces, gyrating mindlessly on his fingers, her head straining back, her nipples peaked, her skin covered with a thin sheen of sweat, and her heart so full, she didn't know it was possible to feel this much for another human being.

As if tasting her and watching her full-body climax wasn't enough to make him rock hard, the tight, tight walls of her pussy clenched his fingers with such force that his dick was literally pulsing for its turn, his mouth watering at the prospect of making love to her.

Tenderly stroking her clit, he watched her face, the way her tongue slipped between her lips to wet them, the way her breasts moved up and down with her shallow breaths, the way her eyes finally opened to show that she'd exchanged emeralds for onyx, the heat of her arousal making them shiny and black.

"Are you okay, *cher*?"

She moaned softly as her eyes rolled back into her head, and Gard grinned, standing up and sliding onto the bed, then pulling her into the curve of his body. Her naked breasts pressing against his T-shirt made him groan softly.

"I'm . . . dead," she murmured, her voice thick and satisfied. Finally she opened her eyes again, and he noted that they were a little greener now, scanning his face in awe. "That was amazing."

"*You're* amazin'," he answered, trailing his fingers down her arm. If he pressed them to his face, they'd smell of her, and the thought made him flinch with longing. He hadn't been with a woman in almost two years, and he didn't know how much longer he could wait.

But he would. If she wasn't ready yet . . . if she was satisfied with what they'd already shared, he would wait. He'd wait forever, if that's what she wanted.

She searched his face, gearing up to say something, then stopping herself.

"Say it," he said, reaching up to caress her cheek.

"The meeting I have this week . . ."

He took a deep breath and sighed. "While you're gone, I'll have my buddy come and look at the security system and—"

"While I'm gone?"

"While you're in LA talkin' to whomever you have to talk to to make a TV show."

She rolled her lips together for a moment, then took a shaky breath. *Gathering her courage. Why? What did she need to tell him?*

"What if I said the meeting was here in Philly? What if I said that . . . all I really want to do is buy this house and ask you to manage it? What if I said I wanted to make my show here, on location, and asked you to consult on it? What if I asked you to move in and live here with me? What would you say?"

"I'd say you don't know me that well."

Her face fell, but her eyes held his as she refuted his words in a rush. "But I feel like I do. I know what I want, and what I want is—"

He continued as if she hadn't spoken. "I'd say you don't know me that well, because if you did, you'd know exactly how I'd answer." He leaned closer to her, resting his forehead against hers. "I'd tell you that runnin' an estate like this would come second nature to me . . . and that consultin' on your show would be a dream job . . . and that movin' in here with you, and having you naked beside me every night and every mornin', and lettin' me keep an eye on you and take care of you and love you . . . well now, that would be the stuff of miracles, Jax."

She'd started crying early into his speech, but now her fingers reached for the button on his jeans with urgency, unfastening it before reaching for his zipper and tugging it down with a satisfying *zzzzzp*.

"Get naked," she said. "I need you. Now."

He rolled onto his back and reached for the waistband of his jeans, bucking up to push them down, then using his feet to free his legs of them. She rolled on top of him, her damp curls covering his erect penis as she pushed his T-shirt to his shoulders. He leaned up and reached for it behind his neck, pulling it off with a yank and wrapping his arms around her body.

Her mouth crashed into his as he reached between them to part the lips of her sex so his dick could slide against her slick, pebbled clit. Her tongue tangled with his and he swallowed her moan as he flipped her to her back so he'd have more control. Knowing how stimulated she was already, he made small movements over the tight bunch of nerves, his pre-cum mixing with the wetness he'd wrought from her before.

"Are you on the pill?" he asked, his voice raspy, and he peppered kisses on her lips, waiting for her to answer.

"Yeah," she said.

"I'm clean, Jax," he said, gazing into her eyes, praying she was too so that there'd be no barrier between them when he slipped into the tight heaven of her body. "I swear to God, I'd never put you in danger."

"I know," she said, smiling as she leaned up to kiss him again.

"What about you?"

"I haven't been with anyone since . . ." Her cheeks colored, and he drew back to look at her.

"Since . . . ?"

"Since college," she said quickly.

He stared at her. "You're twenty-seven."

She nodded.

"You haven't been with anyone for six years?"

"Seven," she whispered.

"Why?" he asked.

"Because it never felt right." She looked up at him, her face calm, her eyes luminous. "And now it does."

"You could have anyone," he said, cradling her face with his hands as he positioned the tip of his erection at the entrance of her sex.

"But all I want," she said, spreading her legs, bending her knees, and reaching to pull his face down to hers, "is you."

He slid forward into the tight, wet heat of her sheath, burying himself to the hilt as she sucked on his tongue and plunged her fingers into his hair, her nails razing his scalp and making him growl as he withdrew from her before thrusting forward again.

His thrusts grew longer and deeper, and her whimpers became cries of pleasure. And finally, when her muscles had tightened around him like a coiled spring, she screamed, "Stay with me, *mon coeur!*" before shuddering with waves of orgasmic bliss.

"I'm here, *cher*. I'm yours!" he cried, spending himself within her beloved body, then holding her close until they both drifted off to sleep.

Chapter 13

There is happiness.

And then there is *joy.*

For the next two weeks, Jax learned all there was to know about joy.

In all her adult life, Jax had never known what it was to wake up in someone's arms every morning after making love throughout the night. She'd never known the playful glances over teeth brushing or the luxury of having a deliciously male perma-date for dinner. She hadn't shared her home with someone in years, and she had forgotten how much she liked having constant company—but even more, *Gard's* constant company. His French terms of endearment, the way he touched her and reached for her, even when they sat side by side reading *Philadelphia Vice*, trading comments and asking each other questions, made her heart swell with love. She missed him when he spent a few hours every day at the Englishes, and the moment he returned, she attacked him with kisses, dragging him up to her shower. They were voracious for each other, their bodies insatiable every night, their hearts loving deeper and stronger with each passing day.

She reached out to the screenwriter of *Philadelphia Vice* and arranged to acquire the script, and she met with a friend of a friend who produced a police procedural in New York. He loved the concept for *Philadelphia Vice* and said he was not only happy to speak to an East Coast studio on her behalf, but he knew of an available showrunner who'd worked on *CSI: New York* for several years and might be interested in taking on *Philadelphia Vice* too. For the first time in months, she felt in charge of her life's direction, felt stronger and more excited, hopeful and passionate . . . and she laid all that positive change at Gardener's feet.

About a week after Gard moved in, he had Le Chateau thoroughly assessed for security needs and made recommendations for cameras and laser sensors, which Jax immediately approved. The first snag in her forward motion, however, came two weeks later, when she was driving to Daisy's house for lunch. Her phone rang and she pressed the button for Bluetooth.

"Hello?"

"Is this Mrs. Rousseau? Mrs. Liliane Rousseau?"

"No," said Jax. "This is her daughter."

"Ah-ha. Well, this is Universal Security, and we have a new order for cameras and surveillance at twelve Blueberry Lane in Haverford, but we require the owner of the house to be present in order to proceed."

"My mother lives in France," said Jax. "But *I* can be prese—"

"We're going to need to get work-order approval from the owner in writing, miss, before we can get started."

Jax was silent for a moment, wiggling uncomfortably in her seat. She'd put off the conversation with her mother about purchasing Le Chateau, but if she truly wanted to make the estate her home, it was time to bite the bullet and talk to her mother about purchasing it. Then she could make all the changes she wanted.

"Hold the order, please," she said. "I'll be in touch soon."

"Thank you, miss. Bye now."

She hung up the call, pulled into Daisy's circular drive-way, and before she lost her nerve, she dialed her mother's number. It was only six o'clock in Paris, three hours before her mother could possibly have evening plans with friends.

"*Bon jour?*"

"*Maman. C'est Jacqueline.*"

"Jacqueline! How are you, darling?"

"I'm well, Mother. How are you?"

"Readjusting to Paris after a month in the states is a nightmare. But it's so good to be home. Promise me, darling, when you get married, it will be here, not there."

Jax sighed. Her mother hadn't handled one iota of Éti-enne's wedding aside from being a snarky pain in the ass about every detail chosen by Kate English. But how like her to act like the burden of the work had been hers. Jax shook her head. *Be nice. You catch more flies with honey.*

"Mother, when you were leaving, you mentioned that you wanted to sell Le Chateau at some point in the future and—"

"But as you pointed out, it's such a hassle. When I'm ready, I'll hire someone to take care of selling it."

"What if I had a buyer for you?"

"Well! I'd say someone's a little miracle worker! Who is it?"

Jax took a deep breath. "Me."

"I'm sorry, darling, but I can't be understanding you right. You? You want to buy Chateau Nouvelle? How ridiculous. Whatever will you do with it?"

"Live in it. I love it here. I would be—"

"But you should be in Hollywood, *chéri*! Where you can make more movies! Where you can be happy."

"But, *Maman*, I *wasn't* hap—"

"My friends are all in love with my daughter, the movie producer! We're going to have a *petite* premiere for your next one. You *belong* in California, darling."

She gulped. This wasn't going well. Her mind raced, trying to come up with a tactic that would appeal to her mother.

"*Maman*, you misunderstand me! I need an East Coast place. A weekend place for parties and relaxing. And Chateau Nouvelle," she grimaced as she said it but was desperate to appeal to her mother, "is so ostentatious, they'll all love it. The pool. The little screening room. The studio. You know Americans."

"Mmmm," her mother hummed. "A weekend place."

"*Oui.* Every major producer has one."

Her mother was silent for a while, then sighed. "*Peut-être.*" Perhaps. "But no. No. I hate it too much, Jacqueline. There is no beauty to it. Find a gorgeous place in New York, darling. A roomy pied-à-terre that looks out over Central Park. Hmm?"

She winced, thinking of the massive stone home that housed not only the best memories of her childhood but now the most cherished of her adulthood too.

"Americans don't require beauty, *chère Maman*. The bigger the better, which makes Le Chateau perfect. It could be a tax write-off for me when it's such a burden for you." She lifted her chin and played into her mother's deepest love: money. "And of course, I would insist on paying full market price."

Her mother chuckled indulgently while Jax winced, silently hating this entire conversation.

"Darling, you've won me over. Yes, of course you can buy the big old thing. Anything for my children." She paused. "Market price, you said?"

"It was last appraised at six million dollars. Would you take seven?" asked Jax.

"Six point nine," said her mother with another benevolent chuckle. "You *are* my daughter, after all. Have it drawn up and send me the papers. You can have your big, ugly house. Now tell me more about your next movie, darling! I want to know everything!"

She blinked, her mind taking a moment to process the fact that her mother had just agreed to sell her Le Chateau! She giggled silently, pounding her feet on the floor of the car in excitement as she and her mother exchanged pleasantries before hanging up.

It was hers! Le Chateau was hers!

Exiting the car, she raced up the marble steps of Daisy's mansion and rang the bell. A young maid showed her outside to a slate terrace, where she found her new friends sipping wine. She spread her arms wide and declared with joy overflowing, "Girls, guess what! I just bought a house!"

When Gardener had taken the job at Haverford Park back in May, he never would have believed the direction his life would take simply by living two doors away from the force of nature that was Jax Rousseau.

But in the several weeks that he'd known her, she'd come to mean much more to him than he could have ever anticipated. And when he walked into Le Chateau after helping Felix for a few hours, the bright excitement on her face made his heart stop, made time stop, and he realized, *I'm in love with you, Jax Rousseau. I'm* desperately *in love with you.*

As the door closed behind him, she raced from her perch on the stairs and jumped into his arms. He caught her with a chuckle of surprise, barely able to catch his breath as she showered kisses on his face and locked her ankles behind his back.

"Jax . . . Jax . . . slow down, *cher*. Tell me what's goin' on with you."

She leaned back, her emeralds sparkling with unspeakable joy. "She said yes!"

"Who said yes?"

"My mother! She said she'd sell Le Chateau to me!"

He was already smiling at her, but now he nodded his head in understanding. "She said yes."

"It's mine, Gard! It's my house! *Our* house!"

"*Your* house, Duchess. But, I'm happy to stay on and manage it for you."

She'd looped her arms around his neck when she jumped him, but now she cupped his cheeks as he carried her to the stairs.

"Where are we going?" she asked, grinning at him, her eyes darkening.

"We're goin' upstairs to your shower, then to your bed, where I'm goin' to spend the next two hours havin' long, hot, multiorgasmic sex with my woman, Haverford's newest homeowner." He reached the top of the stairs and turned left, casting a quick glance at the chandeliers before looking back at Jax. "Any argument?"

She shook her head slowly. "None."

When he got to her room, he let her go, his heart pounding as she slid down his body. "I got to tell you somethin', Jax."

"What?"

"I'm . . ." His eyes caressed her face—her lovely face that hadn't been in his life nearly long enough to have the sorts of feelings that he had for her. And yet they were as fundamental to him as anything else that was certain in his life: that he needed air to breathe, that he needed water to drink, that he loved Jacqueline Rousseau. "You probably already know this, but I want to say it. I want you to hear me say it: I'm in love with you."

Her eyes brightened immediately with tears, and she nodded. "I'm in love with you too."

"I know it's quick."

"Quick for whom?" she asked, reaching for the button of his jeans. "Not for me."

"No?" he asked, letting her slide the jeans down his legs to reveal his hard cock, standing proudly at attention. She reached for it, wrapping her fingers around its throbbing length.

"No. I feel like I've been waiting for you forever."

His eyes shuddered closed as she pumped him, her hand working slowly at first, then faster, and every motion, every movement, was like heaven. His balls started to tighten as she placed her palm on his chest and pushed him back onto the bed.

"Jax, I need to shower . . ."

"I don't mind," she said, looking up at him for just a moment before taking him into her mouth.

"Ahhh!" he groaned, bracing his feet on the floor as she spread his knees and knelt between them, her hand still firmly gripping the base of his erection as her tongue moved lazily over the tip, licking, swirling, and sucking until he thought he'd lose his mind.

When he was on the brink of coming, she stood up, reached under her skirt, pulled down her panties, and then mounted him, straddling his hips as she sunk down onto his slick, rock-hard cock.

"My life didn't begin until the night of my brother's wedding," she said, sighing as she impaled herself on his full length, her nipples highlighted through the fabric of her thin T-shirt and bra. "Until I ran into you."

"*Cher*," he groaned, reaching under her skirt to grasp her hips and hold her still for a moment, wanting to feel the tight walls of her sex throb and quiver around him, to look into her eyes when they were so intimately connected. "*Jacqueline, mon coeur ne bat que pour toi.*"

My heart beats only for you.

A tear slipped from her eye and glided down her cheek as she gazed back at him. "Love me."

He reached for the hem of her shirt and pushed it up, shoving her bra over her breasts to give himself access to them. He took a nipple between his lips, sucking it strongly as she arched her back, meeting his thrusts with moans of pleasure. Sliding his lips to her other breast, he traced a circle around the areola before sucking the nipple into a tight point, only drawing back when she whimpered, plunging her hands into his hair and demanding his lips for a kiss.

He drove up into her body, thrusting deeper and higher with every stroke. His balls tightened as he felt her start to vibrate, and suddenly he stopped thrusting. He needed to slow down because he wanted this moment with her. When they were this close and this intimate, he could see her so clearly, it was almost as though his full sight had been restored. He wanted to look into her eyes as they came together.

Reaching for her chin, he turned her face to his. "Look at me, *cher*. I want to watch you come."

She gasped as he thrust up and held, then drew back. He repeated the action slowly, deliberately, watching her eyes roll back in her head each time he surged forward.

"What's . . . the first . . . rule?" he panted, on the very brink of coming.

"Never look away," she murmured, opening her eyes as he propelled his hips upward and drove into her depths, holding her eyes as the walls of her sex contracted, then pulsated around him, milking him in tight, fast ripples that he could feel to his very soul.

Her forehead dropped onto his shoulder in blissful exhaustion, and he lay back on the bed, still intimately connected with her, turning gently with her so they could lie on their sides and he could stare at her face as she rode out the last waves of her orgasm.

Her skirt was bunched between their stomachs, but he slid her bra and shirt over her head, raising her arms to help her when she whimpered for help. He pulled his T-shirt off so that their chests were bare, then pulled her into his arms, moving gently within her. He was spent, but she still pulsed and trembled around him with tiny aftershocks that made him want her all over again.

Breathing deeply into the curve of his neck, she nestled against him, sighing her pleasure.

He ran his fingers through her long, dark hair.

"So she said yes?" he asked, picking up their conversation from earlier.

"Mm-hm," she murmured.

He didn't know why exactly, but he didn't trust her mother. From what he'd gathered through their many conversations about her family, her mother seemed self-absorbed and self-serving, and a small shiver of doubt sluiced down his spine as he thought about the joy in her face when he walked through the door earlier. *It would hurt her, badly, were she to lose this house,* he thought, holding her closer as her breathing settled into a deep and easy rhythm. He withdrew from her body and smoothed her skirt as best he could, then rested his forehead against hers, closed his eyes, and joined her in sleep.

Ring. Ring ring ring.

Ring. Ring ring ring.

Jax opened her eyes slowly to her dark bedroom, feeling bleary-eyed and tired. Gard snored lightly beside her, and she looked over his shoulder at the clock. Four o'clock. Who the heck was calling at four in the morning?

Ring. Ring ring ring.

Reaching over her sleeping boyfriend, Jax grabbed her phone and looked at the screen. *Maman.*

She sat up against the headboard, pressing talk before putting the phone to her ear. "*Maman*? It's four o'cl—"

"I don't give a *shit* what time it is!"

Jax exhaled a held breath, her blood running cold from the snarl in her mother's voice. "I don't—"

"It's all over the Internet. At least four of my friends have sent me the pictures, Jacqueline."

"What . . . ?"

Her mother cleared her throat. "We don't have a name for the mystery man making out with Jax in the pool, but our sources saw him coming and going from the gardener's cottage at an adjoining estate. Maybe Jacqueline Rousseau is finally getting her field properly plowed."

She gasped in horror. Oh God. The paparazzo had sold the pictures from two weeks ago.

"*Maman*," she started, her voice a sob as memories of being hounded in LA came rushing back to her, making her feel frightened and exposed.

"Fucking the neighbor's gardener? I am the laughing-stock of my friends, Jacqueline!"

"It's not like that . . . I'm in love with—"

"Shut your mouth! Don't you *dare* tell me you're in love with a gardener or I will reach through this phone and strangle you."

"Jax? *Cher*?"

Jax glanced down at Gard, who looked groggy but concerned, and she shook her head at him, placing a finger to her lips, signaling him to be quiet.

"*Maman*, you have to understand—"

"I made some calls, Jacqueline," said her mother in a voice that managed to be both calm and furious. "Your father had the same interest in Hollywood that you do. I called one or two of his old associates, and darling daughter, from what I can gather, you don't have a project right now. No one's seen you out in LA since February!"

"I didn't like being there. I wanted—"

"What? To hide from the world in that garish monstrosity of a mansion?" Her mother paused. "If you think you're still buying that pile of stone, you're delusional. I'm selling it, but *not* to you, and you have one week to leave or I will arrange to have the police remove you. I'm not going to enable this spiral into destruction. Fucking the neighbor's help and living in a mausoleum? No. No, no, no. Not *my* daughter. The house goes on the market tomorrow, and hopefully this is the kick in the ass you need to go back to LA and get your life back on track!"

Tears streamed down her face, and she balled her fists in frustration. "That's not the life I want!"

"Then find a life that doesn't include fucking the neighbor's gardener, you stupid, spoiled girl!"

"You can't do that! You can't tell me how to live my life! You can't . . ." Her voice trailed off in defeat. Somehow she knew her mother had hung up and she was talking into a void. She pulled the phone from her ear to see a blank screen and threw the phone across the room, sobs rising up from within her.

"*Cher* . . ." said Gard, sitting up and pulling her onto his lap, into his arms. "What happened?"

"The pictures of us . . . w-were published online. She's . . . she's a horrible fucking snob, and she's p-pissed about you being a—a gardener. And she won't . . . she won't . . ." She covered her face with her hands, sobbing pitifully against his shoulder. "I have to be out of here in a w-week."

"What?"

"She's s-selling it. She's selling Le Chateau, but sh-she refuses to s-sell it to m-me."

"Because of me?" His arms around her tightened. "Because she objects to me?"

She nodded. "She barely approved of Kate English for Étienne . . . and she wants me to go back to Hollywood. Her *friends* want me to make another movie."

"I see," he said, his voice tight and angry.

She leaned back to look at his face in the moonlight. "You know I don't feel that way! I love you."

He searched her eyes, then gently pushed her head back down to his shoulder. "I know you do, *cher*. I love you too."

"It was all c-coming together," she said, hiccupping. "The sh-show, this house, us. Now it's just . . ."

"Just what . . . ?"

"B-blown to hell!" She sobbed, feeling miserable but still nestling closer to him for comfort. "I have nowhere to live!"

"You can stay with me."

"At the Englishes? God, I couldn't."

"Why not?"

"I . . . ," she leaned back to look at the black of his eyes. "I can't stay in the Englishes' gardener's cottage."

"I'm invitin' you."

"It's one room. It's barely big enough for you." She leaned her cheek back down on his shoulder and sighed, feeling exhausted and defeated. "I'll—I'll go stay with Mad for a while."

"You hate the city."

"I'll have to deal with it for a few weeks."

"And we'll be apart," he said, his body tensing.

"Just until we can figure something out."

"I see," he said again, in that cold, dark tone he'd used before.

She leaned back. "Gard, I love you. I want to be with you."

"Do you, *cher*?"

She nodded. "Of course."

He sighed, then nodded, pulling her back down to the bed and into his arms. Tears still slid down her face as she turned her back to his front and settled her naked body against his.

It felt like there was more to say . . . more that needed to be said, or should be said, but she couldn't think of what. Finally, Gard's voice broke the dark silence.

"Duchess," he said, his voice gruff. "How important is this house to you?"

She considered his question, thinking about her happy childhood memories with her siblings and the blissful few weeks she'd just spent sharing Le Chateau with Gard. She thought about the pool and studio, the gardens and her bedroom. She'd had plans, in her mind, to make a home for herself in Haverford—to make friends with Daisy and Skye, to come home to Le Chateau every day when filming on *Philadelphia Vice* was finished. Having to start over? To pack and find somewhere else to live that held none of the history and happiness of Le Chateau? It hurt.

"When I was walking in the darkness, on the night of my brother's wedding, I was thinking about destiny. Did you know that? I wondered where I was going and what I was doing and what the universe had in store for me. I didn't know then, but I found out a few minutes later . . . the universe had you. You helped me make sense of my life. Everything fell into place because of you." She sniffled softly.

"You were my destiny, Gardener Pierre Thibodeaux. But this house? This house was my dream. I have known happiness here. I would have liked to stay."

"*Ça va, Duchesse*," he said, pressing his lips to the back of her neck. "If you can, sleep. I forgot to tell you, I need to go to New Orleans in the mornin'."

She turned to look at him. "What? Why?"

"Just some family business, *mon coeur*."

Her heart sank. "But . . . I'll be here all alone, and I'm so . . ." *sad*. Then it occurred to her that she was being very selfish. Perhaps his mother or sisters needed him. Perhaps there was a family emergency. "Is everything okay?"

"It will be," he said, kissing her neck again. "I'm sorry about the timin' and so sorry about your house, *cher*. If I could—"

"You can't," she said, turning back around in his arms and closing her burning eyes.

Chapter 14

Jax's arms were laden with bags when she arrived at Mad's place on Thursday night for dinner. She shoved them into a corner of the front vestibule of her sister's apartment, then greeted her siblings: Mad, J.C., and—just back from their honeymoon—Étienne and Kate.

"Where's Gard?" asked Mad. "Wasn't he coming with you?"

Jax accepted a glass of wine from her brother as she sat down next to Kate on the couch in Mad's living room.

"Still in New Orleans," she said.

"I thought he was supposed to be home by today," said Mad, sitting on Jax's other side.

"Me too," said Jax, feeling forlorn.

They'd spoken each day since he'd been gone, and he always told her he loved her when they hung up, but he'd been very mysterious about the purpose of his visit, and she couldn't help but worry that this time apart was badly timed with them being evicted from their love nest.

"What about Thatcher?" asked Jax. "Another conference?"

Mad's face froze for a moment before recovering. "That's right."

"You pressed charges, Jax?" asked Étienne. "Over the pictures?"

Was something going on with Mad? She gave her sister a curious look before turning to Étienne and nodding. "I did. I have my lawyer looking into it. I'm pressing charges for trespassing, and I want the pictures removed from the website."

"Good for you," said her brother, who was a lawyer. "If you run into any snags, let me know."

"Your boyfriend . . . Gard. Will we meet him tomorrow night at Skye Winslow's party?" asked Kate with a hopeful smile.

Jax nodded. "As far as I know, he's supposed to be back by then." She turned to J.C. "Another appraiser came by today to look at Le Chateau. Did you speak to *maman*?"

J.C. nodded, but Jax could tell from his expression that the news wasn't good. "She won't sell to me either. Or Ten or Mad. She said she's selling to a stranger and that you need to get your ass back to LA."

"She's crazy," said Jax with a sniff. "I have no plans to go back to Hollywood. Ever."

"Thatagirl, Jax," said Étienne, raising his glass to her. "So what's your plan?"

She shrugged. "I have to find a realtor, make time to look at houses, find one I want, put a bid on it, move . . . it's exhausting even to think about. For the meantime, I'll stay here."

"I've been meaning to ask," said J.C. "Who else is going to the Winslow thing?"

"I saw Skye yesterday," said Jax. "Looks like Barrett and Emily English, Fitz and Daisy, Stratton and his girlfriend . . ."

"Valeria," supplied Kate.

"Fucking Stratton," muttered Étienne, earning a disapproving look from his wife, who was Stratton's cousin.

"Weston and his fiancée . . . um . . ."

"Molly," said J.C., looking slightly pissed for no good reason.

"Right. Molly. Um, let's see. Brooks and Skye, of course. Cameron and Margaret Winslow. Elise Winslow is in a show on Broadway, so she and Preston can't come, and Christopher can't get away from Washington right now."

"Two Winslows down," said Étienne, winking at J.C.

"The less, the merrier," said Étienne, saluting his brother.

"The Storys?" asked Kate.

Jax nodded. "All four are coming, in addition to Margaret. That was a shocker. I didn't even know Alice lived around here anymore."

Étienne gave J.C. a look. "Oh, *Alice* is coming. Did you hear that, Jean-Christian? Alice!"

"Shut the fuck up, Ten."

"What about the Amblers?" asked Mad.

"Bree, yes. Sloane yes."

Mad groaned. "Sloane? Ugh."

J.C. perked up. "Sloane was always hot."

"And easy," added Étienne.

Kate gave her husband a dirty look.

"Not that I ever sampled the goods, *chaton*."

"What's Sloane up to these days?" asked J.C.

"She owns an antique store," said Mad.

Jax turned to her sister. "You keep in touch with her?"

"N-not really," said Mad, standing up quickly. "J.C. needs a refill."

"What about Cort, Jax?" asked Étienne with a shit-eating grin.

"As far as I know, he's coming."

"New boyfriend and old boyfriend all in one place, huh?"

"Shut up, Ten," said Mad, coming back into the living room with a bottle of wine to refresh everyone's glass.

"Oh my God!" exclaimed Kate. "That's right! I almost forgot you two used to date."

"Ancient history," said Mad, giving Jax an anxious smile.

Jax nodded in agreement. "Dark Ages-ancient."

"And Dash?" asked J.C.

Jax shrugged. "No idea. He never got back to Skye."

"That's because he's in Calcutta," said Mad. When everyone in the room turned to her to find out how the hell she knew that, she shrugged, then bustled back toward the kitchen. "I need to check on dinner."

"I'm sorry about Le Chateau," said Kate, slipping closer to Jax on the couch as J.C. and Étienne started a conversation about European soccer.

Jax sighed. "I should have seen it coming."

"Your mother is . . . challenging."

"She wasn't very nice to you, was she? The month before the wedding when she was visiting, I could tell she was being a bitch. I'm sorry I didn't intercede more. I was too wrapped up in my own life to see how awful she was."

"My own parents weren't exactly a walk in the park," said Kate. "Let's just assume I can handle difficult parents. Yours *and* mine."

"She just has certain ideas about our futures," said Jax. "And they don't include dating 'the help.'"

"You new boyfriend . . . is he really a gardener?"

Jax felt her lips twitch into a smile. "Sort of. He was a detective, but he was injured two years ago and doesn't see as well as he used to. He had to retire."

"Injured?" asked Kate.

"Shotgun blast too close to his face. Compromised his eyesight."

"I'm sorry," said Kate. "I hope you don't mind my asking, but if he's partially blind, how exactly does he garden?"

She thought about the times she'd watched him, kneeling in the soil, close to the earth. "He takes his time. His father was a landscaper."

"You really like him," said Kate, her voice a little lower, her blue eyes serious.

Jax nodded, leaning closer to Kate. "I *more than* like him. I love him."

Kate nodded, giving Jax a sweet smile. "I can tell. I just didn't want to say it . . . in case you didn't realize it yet."

"My mother will flip if he ends up being the one."

Kate cocked her head to the side. "But be honest, Jax—do you really care?"

"No," she said, shaking her head. "I just—I would have really liked to have Le Chateau, you know? She never loved it, but I always have."

"Of course you do. It's your home."

"Yeah," said Jax. "Or it *was*. But for the first time in a long time, I know where I'm headed. I'm staying here in Philly with all of you. And Gard. I'm making my TV show. My mother's not in charge of my life. I am. And I'm not going to let fear keep me in a box anymore."

"Good for you, Jax," said Kate, taking her hand and squeezing it. "Good for you. And when you're ready to go house hunting, give me a call. I think Étienne and I are going to be in the market for a house soon too. We can look together!"

Jax raised an eyebrow. "But Ten loves the city."

"Mmm," said Kate, looking over at her husband with a twinkle in her eye. "He does."

"Dinner's ready," said Mad, coming from the kitchen and looking flustered.

Between Mad's weird inside knowledge of the Amblers' whereabouts and Kate's sudden interest in house hunting, Jax felt like she was missing big pieces of these conversations, but J.C. put his arm around her shoulder to usher her into dinner, and talk quickly shifted to Étienne and Kate's Mooréa honeymoon. And the moment to pull Mad or Kate aside slipped away in the inevitable hubbub of a family reunited.

"Just get it done," said Gardener, slapping his palm on Flannery "Flint" Lenox's massive mahogany desk. "I've been here for three danged days. This is ridiculous. It's *my* money."

"Yes, indeed, Mr. Thibodeaux, it is," said Flint, sarcasm heavy in his voice. "But your daddy left me very specific instructions, and I am *not* willin' to dishonor his good name by lettin' y'all buy some Yankee piece of prop'ty that hasn't been appraised to my standards, y'hear?"

"I've *seen* the house. I've been *livin'* there. I'd say seven million sounds about right." Gard clenched his jaw, sitting back in the black wicker guest chair as sweat dripped in rivulets down the sides of his face, and gave Flint Lenox a dark look.

"And don't be glarin' at me none either, son. I knowed you since you was in short pants." Mr. Lenox adjusted his glasses, then picked up his phone, dialing a number. "Hey, darlin', it's Flint here. You heard from that appraiser up north yet? Hmm? Unh. Well, now. No, no. I'm glad to know it. Yes, ma'am. How 'bout you fax that report to me? Thanks, darlin'. Oh, yes, ma'am, we'll see y'all at the Baptist picnic Sunday next. Wouldn't miss it. Best to 'ole Humph too."

Gard gave Flint an exasperated look.

"The report come in and I was right. Ain't worth seven million. Worth closer to six. Maybe even five point five in this market."

"So call her and offer six. I want the contents included. She wants to unload it, right?"

"Yes, sir, from what the broker tells me."

"So?"

"So it's . . ." Flint checked his watch. ". . . seven o'clock in Paris. You want to call the lady this evenin'?"

"Hell, yes," said Gard. "I need to get back to Philadelphia."

"Dang, you adopted some Northern ways, son, barely restin' a moment to breathe."

"Flint?" said Gard, trying for a more patient tone. "Please make the call?"

". . . in a danged rush," said Flint under his breath, dialing the number of Liliane Rousseau's real estate broker in Pennsylvania. "Hello? Well, hello, there. Flannery Lenox here." He chuckled. "Aren't you sweet to remember me?" More chuckling, which just about made steam pour from Gard's ears. "That client I called you about yesterday . . . well, he's ready to make an offer, but I should warn you, it's under the askin' price." Flint paused, nodding at whatever the broker was saying as he turned to take an incoming fax off the machine. "Yes, ma'am, I have the new appraisal here. Uh-huh. I can fax it up to your office. Looks like the property has devalued a bit over the past thirty years. Bull market." He turned back to the machine, slipped the fax in the top tray, and dialed a number. "Comin' to you right now. Appraiser's the one you recommended." He paused again, looking at Gard as he listened. "We're thinkin' six as-is, contents included. Yes, ma'am. Fifty percent down." He raised an eyebrow and his mouth wobbled into a smile. "I know twenty percent is customary, but my buyer is . . . motivated. He's set on fifty. She does, huh? Tell her Gardener Pierre Thibodeaux of the Nawlins Thibodeauxs. Yes, ma'am. Fine Acadian family." He took a deep breath and sighed. "Buyer says he needs an answer today, so would you be a darlin' and give her a call? I know, I know, but he's eager to get matters settled. Uh-huh. Bindin' escrow agreement today. Tomorrow at the latest." He looked up at Gard and shrugged, then suddenly his face brightened. "Well, that's just fine. We'll wait to hear from you. Thank you, kindly. Uh-huh. Bye now."

He hung up the phone and gave Gard a sour look. "She's callin' the Rousseau woman in Paris, and she'll call us back after they've spoken."

Gard nodded. "That's fine. You think she'll call back today?"

"Can't tell what she'll do, but why don't you go visit with your mama a spell and I'll call you if she agrees."

Standing up, Gard offered his hand to Flint. "Thanks for this."

Flint frowned at him but took his hand. "Never did understand why you wanted to put down roots up there, Gard. This is a big commitment, to buy a house."

"I know what I'm doin', Flint."

"Well, I surely hope so. You're going to deplete damn near all of your trust, and you'll be saddled with a thirty-year mortgage, taxes, maintenance. Some might call this insanity, son."

Gard put his hands on his hips and grinned. "How much you love Miss Maisy?"

Flint lifted his jowly chin, pointing a finger at Gard. "You know how I feel about that woman. Met Maisy-Jane on a Tuesday. Proposed on a Wednesday. Had to wait a danged year for her to say yes, but I never wavered. Not once. She was it for me, and I knew it from the word go."

"Some might call that insanity, son," he said quietly.

"Dang it, but you always had a smart mouth," said Flint, shaking his head back and forth. "Go on and get out of here. I'll call you if she says yes."

"Call me anyway, Flint."

"How high you willin' to go, Gardener?"

"As high as it takes, sir. That house is mine."

Flint nodded. "I hope she's worth it."

"She is, Flint," he said, without a hint of doubt in his heart or mind. "She surely is."

By Friday, the fourth morning of Gard's absence, Jax started to feel uneasy about him. A night in New Orleans had turned into two, into three, and damn it, but she needed him. Her mother had sent a terse e-mail advising her that tomorrow the men were coming to turn off the water, electricity, and gas, and a moving company was scheduled to start moving the furniture to a storage unit near Philadelphia until Liliane could decide what was to be done with it.

Tonight was Skye Winslow's party. Tomorrow morning, she'd move in with Mad.

But the longer she went without seeing Gard, the more disconnected she felt from him, and there were even moments when she wondered if he'd gotten what he wanted from her, had some fun, and now moved on. Her heart splintered to imagine that their exchanges of love hadn't meant anything to him, and it didn't feel right to even wonder about it. She'd looked into his eyes as they'd shared the most intimate connection two people could possibly share. He loved her. She was certain of it.

So what was he doing in Louisiana, and why was he being so cagey about it? When she asked what he was up to, all he'd say is "family business" and change the conversation back to her. It was making her crazy.

And sad.

Well, she was sad anyway. On Tuesday, her mother had fired the domestic staff with generous severances, and saying good-bye to Mrs. Jefferson on Tuesday afternoon had not been easy for Jax. In fact, none of this was easy for Jax. She just wished that she could have Gard's arms around her as she fell asleep for the final time at Le Chateau tonight. She just wished he could hold her as she said her good-byes to the house she loved and cried her eyes out on the drive to Mad's house tomorrow morning.

After a lonely breakfast, the front doorbell rang, and Jax answered it to find two men from Million-Dollar Movers on her front step.

"Here to make a final assessment for tomorrow's job," said one of the men, and Jax's eyes filled with tears as they stepped inside with clipboards. She was due to help decorate for the party next door at noon, but she wondered about going early.

She took her phone out of her pocket to text Skye but found a message waiting:

GARD: Business completed. Will be on the two o'clock flight. Home at six. Wait for me.

She took a deep, ragged breath and sighed, hot tears of relief brightening her eyes and making the words blur on the screen.

JAX: Party starts at six. Do you want to meet me there?
GARD: No. Meet me at home, cher. We need to talk.

Jax flinched at these words, which she'd only ever heard twice, in the context of boyfriends breaking up with her: once in high school when Cort Ambler had pulled the plug on their romance and once again in college.

She tried to stay calm.

JAX: About what?
GARD: It's important. We'll talk in person. See you later, Duchess.

Her heart plummeted, and she sat down on the grand staircase, letting the phone drop to the red carpet by her thigh as tears coursed down her cheeks. He was breaking up with her. She'd bet her life on it. She couldn't offer him a job managing Le Chateau. She was temporarily moving in with her sister. Her life was at sixes and sevens. Hell, since the moment he'd met her, her life probably looked like a train wreck. It was a good time for a clean break, she thought pathetically. And he was taking it.

"Uh, miss?"

She looked up to see one of the Million-Dollar Movers standing in front of her, his clipboard by his side.

She sniffled, swiping her tears away. "Yes?"

"We'll be going now."

"You're finished already?"

The man shook his head, holding up his cell phone. "Nope. Job was just canceled. I guess you got a buyer for your house. Congratulations!"

"A buyer?" she repeated.

He nodded. "Yep. We were told not to move the furniture."

"Why not?"

He shrugged. "Don't know. Best guess is that the buyer wants it all. You have a good day, miss."

She watched in stunned disbelief as he and his partner headed to the front door, closing it firmly behind them.

Not only had someone purchased her childhood home, but they'd purchased everything in it. Which meant that all the things that reminded her of her father and siblings would belong to someone else. All her mother's stupid Parisian knickknacks, the grandfather clock in the ballroom, the desk where her father wrote checks, the gym where she fell in love. It would all belong to someone else.

Everything was ending or falling apart, and even for Jax, who was a relatively strong woman, it was too much. Placing her hand over her heart, she looked around the foyer, holding back her sobs for as long as she could, then letting them break forth as she walked up the stairs to the fleeting sanctuary of her bedroom.

Air travel is not a simple task when you're legally blind, thought Gard, who had no choice but to state his disability when he booked his tickets and arrange to have someone accompany him from the gate to the taxi stand at the Philadelphia International Airport. And while he still hated the feeling of being dependent on someone else, the reality was that with Jax's help, he was coming to accept the hand he'd been dealt in life. She didn't treat him like a disabled person. She didn't patronize him or look down at him. In fact, it was her confidence in him had given him the courage to get on a plane in the first place. Her confidence in him and the fact that he wasn't going to let Liliane-fucking-Rousseau, or anyone else, break his woman's heart. No, sir. Her heart belonged to him, and he took care of what was his. Gard was learning that there were ways to keep someone safe and protect them that had nothing to do with being—as Jax had put it—a "Neanderthal goon with a club." Sometimes keeping someone safe was about keeping their heart safe and making their life easier. Sometimes it was just about making sure that you stood as a buffer between them and any ugliness in the world, even if that ugliness issued from their own mother.

The negotiation hadn't been simple. Liliane had asked for a ridiculous and astronomical eight million dollars. Gard had volleyed back with six point three. She had come back with seven. He had offered six point four. She had finally come back with six point six and they'd settled and the house had gone to contract. From his trust, he'd withdrawn three point three million dollars for a fifty percent down payment on Le Chateau, which was presently being held in escrow with the First Bank of Philadelphia. After disclosures and inspections, they'd close the escrow, the down payment would be made, and Gardener Thibodeaux would be the owner of Le Chateau, including a brand-new thirty-year mortgage with payments he'd never be able to make on his own. However, if Jax was still willing to offer him the job of estate manager, his salary would cover it.

I've learned a lot about faith over the past few days, he thought as the taxi zoomed toward Haverford. He'd also learned a lot about the depth of his love for Jax and the hope he had for their future together. From the very beginning, he'd known she was different, singular. But until four days ago, he hadn't yet learned the lengths to which his heart was willing to go to secure what belonged to him. He hadn't known that falling in love with her meant that he'd do anything—beyond reason or common sense, beyond prudence—to make her happy. And since money didn't mean a great deal to him but Le Chateau meant a great deal to her, it made sense to him to buy it for her, to keep it safe for her, to protect her heart, to make her happy. In fact, nothing—not anything in the whole world—could possibly make more sense to him than that.

As the taxi approached the gates of Le Chateau, they opened for him, and his heart leapt because it meant she was waiting for him as he'd requested. The contract was folded in his blazer pocket, and all that was left was to tell her this:

Le Chateau is yours.

Jax had already dressed for the party in a blue-and-white pinstriped sundress and white heeled sandals. She had a silver chain around her neck and a matching bracelet, and her hair was down, tumbling in waves around her shoulders. She'd checked herself in the mirror ten times, much good it would do her. If he'd decided that they were over, she refused to beg. In fact, she'd opened the gates so that she could step outside and meet him. Once the conversation started going south, it would be easier to tell him to leave if they were already outside.

Her hands trembled as she rose from her father's desk. Her heart had broken this afternoon when she discovered Le Chateau had been sold, but she feared that losing Gard would shatter it into a million pulverized pieces that could never be put back together again. It had been hard to think of leaving Le Chateau, but with Gard by her side, it had been bearable. Now? She may as well return to LA. She couldn't possibly be more miserable there than here without him.

Stepping outside, she walked to the top of the steps that led to the driveway and stood there with her hands clasped before her. As the taxi pulled up in front of the house, she blinked her eyes and held her breath, unprepared for the strong wave of pure, unadulterated love she felt for the man who exited from the backseat and stood before her as the car pulled away.

Tall and impossibly beautiful in jeans, a white button-down shirt, and a navy-blue blazer, his thick, dark-blond hair was wavy and tousled, and a few days of beard growth covered his strong jaw. She braced herself to hear his voice—to hear the richness of his lightly accented baritone when he greeted her.

"Jax?" he said, looking up at her from several feet away.

"*C'est moi*," she answered softly, thinking that her heart really *hadn't* broken today after all. It still beat inside her chest, as strong and solid as ever. There was a difference between a sad heart and a broken one. Losing Le Chateau had made her sad. Losing Gard would break her.

In fact, if this was the end for them, she didn't care about Le Chateau anymore. She didn't care about *Philadelphia Vice* or staying near her family. If she never got to see him exit a car headed for her arms again, frankly, she didn't care about anything. Everything—every last thing in her life—would feel meaningless if this was the end of her time with him.

She gulped, drawing her hands into fists by her sides. "How was your trip?"

"What's between you and me?" he asked, letting his duffel bag slide from his shoulder onto the gravel of the driveway as he squinted to see.

She flinched, the double meaning of the question striking profoundly at her heart. "Umm . . ."

"*Cher*," he said, "are you okay?"

"What do you want to talk to me about?" she asked in a rush.

"Let's go inside and sit down," he suggested.

She clenched her teeth together and closed her eyes. "No."

"Why not?"

She worked hard not to sob. "Please. Please just say it."

He squinted up at her again. "What's between you and me?"

"Nothing. Some gravel. A few flagstones. Three steps."

Carefully making his way from the driveway to where she stood, she could tell when she came into focus for him, because his eyes softened with such tenderness, it made her want to weep. And for the first time, she wondered if maybe he didn't want to break up . . . if maybe there was something else on his mind.

He reached for her, drawing her into his strong arms and burying his face in her hair. "I missed you. I missed you. Lord, how I missed you, *cher*."

And then, because she was so relieved, the dam broke loose, and all the tears she'd been swallowing started to fall as she threw her arms around his neck, clutching him to her, her fingers digging into the skin at the back of his neck. He found her lips with his, kissing her madly as he pulled her impossibly closer. When she was breathless and boneless, he leaned back and kissed her cheeks, her nose, and each eyelid.

"Don't cry, Duchess."

"It's been a terrible week," she said, leaning against the solid strength of his body. "How was your visit?"

"Next time, you come with me," he said.

"Where?" she asked, smiling through her tears. "Nawlins?"

"Anywhere. Everywhere. Four nights was an eternity."

Standing in his arms, she searched his face. "You scared me. I thought maybe—"

"What?" he asked, his forehead creasing.

"When you said we needed to talk, I thought you wanted to break up."

His head jerked back and forth. "What? Why? Why would you think that?"

"Your sudden trip. It kept getting extended. You wouldn't tell me what was going on."

"Oh, *mon coeur*. I didn't want to get your hopes up," he said, reaching up to caress her face. "I didn't want to say anythin' until I was sure."

"Sure of what?"

"Do you love me?" he asked, his eyes searching hers.

"More than anything," she answered.

"I love you too. Do you trust me?"

"Yes." She clutched him tighter. "I'm sorry I doubted you."

"I only want to be with you," he said, "forever, to be exact, but you don't have to say yes to forever today. Today I just need . . . well, thirty years or so."

"Thirty years?" she asked, searching his face as an excited giggle bubbled up inside of her. "What do you mean?"

He took a deep breath, holding her a little closer. "I couldn't bear to see you so sad, *cher*. Not when it was within my power to make you happy again."

"Within your power . . . ?"

"My father was successful. Very successful and very rich when he died. He left substantial trusts for me and my sisters. A trust that I have mostly ignored up until now." Suddenly, he leaned down and kissed her—tenderly, lovingly—and when he drew back, his eyes were conflicted: intense, excited, just on the brink of troubled. "But my duchess needed her castle."

She whimpered softly. "Her . . . ?"

With one hand, he reached into the breast pocket of his blazer, withdrawing a folded piece of paper, which he presented to her. She reached for the paper, unfolding it as he continued. "I bought Le Chateau for you, Jacqueline. I bought you a house, your house—well, I guess, actually, *our* house."

The paper before her blurred from the tears filling her eyes, and she blinked, letting them fall at will. He'd bought her Le Chateau. He'd bought her everything. *He* was the buyer who had stopped the movers from disassembling her beloved house.

"Gard," she sobbed, falling back into his arms, clutching the contract in her hands behind his neck.

"I want you to have it . . . I *need* you to have it. You can buy it from me if you want it in your name, or we can . . ."

"*From* you?" she asked, leaning back to look up into his face, unable to keep the combination of beaming smile and onslaught of tears at bay. "I don't want it unless you're here *with* me."

His eyes were bright with tears, and he took a deep, jagged breath, nodding at her as he smiled back.

"*Ça va*," he said, reaching for her cheek. "Then it's ours, Duchess. Our home."

She leaned up to capture his lips, holding the contract in one hand and threading her fingers through his hair with the other. He groaned into her mouth, holding her tighter, his tongue sliding against hers, reacquainting itself with her taste and texture as she did the same. Finally he leaned away, resting his forehead against hers.

"You're happy."

"You make me happy," she whispered through her tears.

"One problem solved. We're not homeless anymore." As he drew back from her, he looked up at their new house. "There is one other little problem, though, *cher*."

"There couldn't be. Life just got totally perfect."

"No, there is. *Two* problems, in fact. The first is that I'm mostly broke now. My trust is just about empty, and I own this big, 'ole house in Pennsylvania. The second is that I don't have a job anymore, because Felix decided he needed full-time help. So I was just wonderin' . . . do you know of anyone who might have some long-term, full-time work for me in Pennsylvania?"

She knew her smile was blinding. She knew it because she could see it reflected in his eyes, in the way they shone with love for her.

"Long-term like thirty years, maybe?"

He nodded, grinning at her. "'Zactly."

"Because I was thinking I needed some more self-defense lessons . . . and an estate manager . . . did I mention I'm making a TV show about cops here in Philadelphia? I am, and I could use an advisor . . . though what I really need— since you brought up the subject of forever, *mon coeur*—is someone to *spend* forever with."

"You know what we could do? When you're ready, we could roll up all those jobs into one, Duchess."

She nodded, giggling softly before asking, "And call it something like . . . duke?"

"Or we could just go with husband," he said, chuckling as he drew her back into the safe haven of his arms and kissing her truly, madly, deeply because . . .

. . . sometimes friends do that.

THE END

The Rousseaus continues with ...

MARRY ME MAD

THE ROUSSEAUS, BOOK #2

THE ROUSSEAUS
(Part III of the Blueberry Lane Series)

Jonquils for Jax
Marry Me Mad
J.C. and the Bijoux Jolis

Turn the page for a sneak peek of *Marry Me Mad*!

Red and green martinis, thought Madeleine Rousseau, checking out the colorful cocktails that greeted the guests who arrived at the Winslows' sailing-themed summer party. *Port and starboard. Clever.*

Picking up a green martini, she took a sip as she stepped onto the slate patio. Out on the lawn, there was a full-size movie screen, and the Winslows had rented comfortable theater-style seats that were set up in five or six rows of four chairs each. A movie night under the stars. It was such a charming idea, Mad couldn't help but smile . . . until she noticed Cortlandt Ambler hurrying up the marble steps toward her, his unruly dirty-blond hair brushing his shoulders and blue-gray eyes trained, like lasers, on hers.

The sleeves of his white button-down dress shirt were rolled up to reveal intricate tattoos that covered his forearms, ending sharply at his wrists. Other guests at the party would have to guess if the tattoos rose higher than his elbows, but Mad knew the swirled designs by heart. She knew that they rose to his shoulders, some trailing down his back and others connected to more ink on his chest. Her fingers twitched with a sensory memory of his skin, of hours spent mapping the contours of his beautiful body.

Her lips parted to speak, but her breathing hitched and a lump in her throat trapped all of the words she longed to say.

"Hi," he breathed, his eyes trailing tenderly over her face.

"I thought you weren't coming," she said, her voice perilously close to a sob.

"I wasn't planning to and then . . ."

She gulped, willing herself not to cry.

"How are you?" he asked and the familiarity of his soft, gritty voice made her heart throb, made her eyes burn.

She lifted her chin, trying on bravado . . . "Absolutely fine. How are you?" . . . and finding it a poor fit.

"You don't have to lie to me, Mad." He leaned closer. "How's your asshole boyfriend?"

"Fine," she said softly, looking away.

Cort's voice was tight with anger as he flicked a glance to the double doors that led from the main house onto the terrace. "Is he here with you?"

"He's at a conference."

"Another *conference*," spat Cort.

More and more people were greeting the Winslows, spilling outside. Mad looked around quickly for Jax before turning to face him. "People make mistakes."

"It wasn't a mistake, Mad."

His meaning was clear and it twisted her heart, but Jax would be here any minute, and with the uncanny insight of a twin, she would know way too much if she caught Mad talking to Cort. Their emotions were running way too high to conceal. She had to get away from him. Now. The sooner the better.

"It was good to see you, Cort. I have to go."

As she turned to leave, he grabbed her wrist, his fingers gentle but still somehow searing, and suddenly every nerve ending in her body was concentrated in her right forearm. His long fingers wrapped around her slim wrist with ease, and Mad had to bite her bottom lip to keep from sighing. She'd missed him so desperately.

"Mad, please," he begged her, his voice a mere whisper.

She turned to look up at him, her eyes caressing his face without her permission—the omnipresent dark-blond scruff on his jaw, the high, regal cut of his cheekbones, the long, dark lashes that shielded his blue-gray eyes.

"It's not my fault I was there that night," he said, his voice an intense growl near her ear as she turned away from him.

Her eyes filled with tears and she knew she would sob if she tried to speak.

He moved closer to her and she could feel the heat of his body, his hot breath kissing her neck. "It's not my fault I can't forget it."

"Please," she whispered as her eyes fluttered closed.

"It's not my fault that I fell in—"

"Skye!" exclaimed Jax, entering the terrace several yards behind them and kissing Skye Winslow hello. "You got the perfect weather for tonight!"

Something surged inside of Mad. Something even stronger than the intense longing she felt for the man who held her wrist . . . who still held her heart.

"We agreed," said Mad, jerking her arm away from his grasp and opening her eyes to look up at him. "We agreed to say good-bye and walk away."

"What if I can't?" he asked, his voice thick with a heartache she shared but managed to conceal.

"I'm sorry," she whispered.

Then she turned and walked away from him, heading toward her sister as fast as her feet could carry her.

**Look for *Marry Me Mad* at your
local bookstore or buy online!**

Other Books by Katy Regnery

A MODERN FAIRYTALE
(Stand-alone, full-length, unconnected romances inspired by classic fairy tales.)

The Vixen and the Vet
(inspired by "Beauty and the Beast")
2014

Never Let You Go
(inspired by "Hansel and Gretel")
2015

Ginger's Heart
(inspired by "Little Red Riding Hood")
2016

Dark Sexy Knight
(inspired by "The Legend of Camelot")
2016

Don't Speak
(inspired by "The Little Mermaid")
2017

Swan Song
(inspired by "The Ugly Duckling")
2018

ABOUT THE AUTHOR

***New York Times* and *USA Today* bestselling author Katy Regnery** started her writing career by enrolling in a short story class in January 2012. One year later, she signed her first contract and Katy's first novel was published in September 2013.

Twenty-five books later, Katy claims authorship of the multi-titled, *New York Times* and *USA Today* bestselling Blueberry Lane Series, which follows the English, Winslow, Rousseau, Story, and Ambler families of Philadelphia; the six-book, bestselling A Modern Fairytale series; and several other standalone novels and novellas.

Katy's first modern fairytale romance, *The Vixen and the Vet*, was nominated for a RITA® in 2015 and won the 2015 Kindle Book Award for romance. Katy's boxed set, *The English Brothers Boxed Set*, Books #1–4, hit the *USA Today* bestseller list in 2015, and her Christmas story, *Marrying Mr. English*, appeared on the list a week later. In May 2016, Katy's Blueberry Lane collection, *The Winslow Brothers Boxed Set*, Books #1–4, became a *New York Times* E-Book bestseller.

In 2016, Katy signed an agreement with Spencer Hill Press. As a result, her Blueberry Lane paperback books will now be distributed to brick-and-mortar bookstores all over the United States.

Katy lives in the relative wilds of northern Fairfield County, Connecticut, where her writing room looks out at the woods, and her husband, two young children, two dogs, and one Blue Tonkinese kitten create just enough cheerful chaos to remind her that the very best love stories begin at home.

Sign up for Katy's newsletter today: www.katyregnery.com!

Connect with Katy

Katy LOVES connecting with her readers and answers every e-mail, message, tweet, and post personally! Connect with Katy!

Katy's Website: http://katyregnery.com
Katy's E-mail: katy@katyregnery.com
Katy's Facebook Page: https://www.facebook.com/KatyRegnery
Katy's Pinterest Page: https://www.pinterest.com/
    katharineregner
Katy's Amazon Profile: http://www.amazon.com/
    Katy-Regnery/e/B00FDZKXYU
Katy's Goodreads Profile: https://www.goodreads.com/author/
    show/7211470.Katy_Regnery

4907

CPSIA information can be obtained at www.ICGtesting.com
Printed in the USA
LVOW11s1908130816

500149LV00003B/4/P

9 781633 920927